BROKEN

By

Susan Elle

For

Ursula Publishing UK

Other Books by Susan Elle

The Sara Colson Trilogy includes
Sara's Child
Sara's Loss
Sara's Shame
All the above also available as audio books.

Catherine Colson-Sayers Investigations
CCS Investigations : Bk 1 : Missing
CCS Investigations : Bk 2 : The Chosen
CCS Investigations : Bk 3 : Travis
CCS Investigations : Bk 4 : Deleted
CCS Investigations : Bk 5 : Mind Games, due out end
Aug 2015, twice the length of previous books.

Tempest
Broken

Love, Lies & Consequences Trilogy
Love : Bk1
Lies : Bk2
Consequences : Bk3

Langdon Trilogy
Heart & Home : Bk1
Heart of a Lion : Bk2
Heart of Stone : Bk3

www.susan-elle.com

Table of Contents

INSPIRATIONAL QUOTES

There is, in every true woman's heart, a spark of heavenly fire, which lies dormant in the broad daylight of prosperity, but which kindles up and beams and blazes in the dark hour of adversity.

Washington Irving

You gain strength, courage, and confidence by every experience in which you really stop to look fear in the face. You are able to say to yourself, 'I lived through this horror. I can take the next thing that comes along.'

Eleanor Roosevelt

PROLOGUE

For just a second of time the quarry falls eerily silent. Not a single man or beast appears to move or even breath. A 50 ton dumper truck, with wheels taller than a man, has slid off the side of one of the cut levels and tumbled all the way down to the quarry bed, the monster coming to rest on its side.

"Get that bloody crane over here now!" Lucas Forrester races over to the horrific scene shouting orders to his men as he goes. "Craig, get on the blower and get an ambulance out here pronto – no one gets out of an accident like this without serious injuries!"

Lucas' site foreman rushes to his side, bringing half a dozen experienced quarry workers with him. "Got a plan, boss?" Hank Fisher asks hurriedly.

"We can't move the truck in case the driver needs his

spine stabilising...," Lucas states as they stride towards the monster truck, "...so I'm going to use the crane to winch me onto the cab, then I can assess the driver's condition."

Turning to his foreman, Lucas asks for the driver's identity.

"It's young Davey," Hank growls out as he pushes a hand back through his thick thatch of salt and pepper hair.

His eyes full of suspicion, Lucas stops abruptly and brings Hank to a jarring halt beside him. "Tell me he was clean!" Lucas demands, his slate grey eyes darkening like a storm about to break.

Nodding, Hank stands up for Davey, "He's been clean for going on 6 months now. I personally accompanied him to all his group sessions and periodic blood tests that he had to prove he wasn't using. I don't believe he would have let you down, he has a lot of respect for you." Hank feels very protective of Davey; he'd been charged with either getting the young man clean or firing his arse!

Now he's praying that his belief in the lad is justified and hoping that Davey comes out of this alive!

Staring hard into his foreman's eyes, Lucas finally gives a nod, "Good enough!" Then Lucas waves the approaching crane into position.

A massive hook dangles at the end of a supersized

chain. "Sid, can you hoist me up onto the cab?"

"No probs, boss," the crane driver calls back.

Lucas climbs onto the hook and is slowly swung up and over the overturned truck.

Jumping down onto the side of the driver's cab, Lucas waves at the crane driver to let him know he's ok...then takes his first look at the driver.

Can't see his face. He could just be out cold...and no wonder after that fall! Damn it, Davey, don't you dare be dead! Just hang on in there!

Now that the crane has turned off its engine the eerie silence resumes. Men and women from all over the quarry have gathered to watch the ghastly scene.

In the history of the quarry, nothing like this has ever happened before. Every heart present is beating fit to burst waiting for some resolution to the nightmare that is unfolding, and the people they belong to are almost suspended in time as the minutes tick by without anyone noticing.

Climbing carefully down, Lucas calls out to Davey but gets no response. "I'm coming down to you, Davey, and an ambulance is already on the way." As he comes alongside the young man, Lucas lets out an ironic chuckle, "You know, if you needed some time off work you could have just asked. This is taking skiving to the extreme...don't you think?"

But Davey still doesn't answer and now Lucas can see why. "Christ Almighty, Davey...what the hell did you go and do?"

A young man, in the prime of his life, lies still and unseeing behind the wheel. The silence is now oppressive, the magnitude of the accident hitting Lucas square in the gut and he has to breathe deeply to force back the claustrophobic feel of the cab.

Putting a gentle hand over his lifeless eyes, Lucas draws Davey's eyelids down with a heavy sigh. "I'll make sure your wife is taken care of son," he tells the young man. "But right now, we have to get you out of here."

CHAPTER ONE

Sitting across from his foreman, Lucas sips at his mug of strong tea in contemplative silence.

The ambulance has taken Davey's body to the hospital, the paramedic having pronounced him dead at the scene. Now the aftermath is unfolding, the quarry slowly getting back down to business and the magnitude of what has just happened settles in.

How the hell do I tell his wife that she's now a widow? She can't be more than early twenties...Davey was only 27. Bloody hell, that's way too young to be dead!

"It was no one's fault," Hank finally states when he sees the way his boss is torturing himself.

"Really...," Lucas asks sceptically, "...and is that what I'm supposed to tell his wife?!"

Letting out a long low sigh, Hank shakes his head, "No.

And I'll tell her about Davey," he offers. "I got to know her a little bit when I was taking Davey to his substance abuse support group."

But Lucas won't hear of it. As owner of the quarry he gets the perks of the job, the nice profit that comes with a meticulously organised business that usually runs like a well-oiled machine. Now he has to take his lumps, face up to the downside of being the boss and take responsibility for telling a young wife that her husband will never again walk into their home, share her life or her bed, that he died while working for Lucas Forrester.

"That's my job. As unpleasant as I'm sure it will be I won't shirk that responsibility. I want to make sure she understands that I'll help her out in any way she needs."

On the drive to Davey's house, Lucas tries to think how best to phrase the bad news he is about to impart. But everything he thinks of sounds trite and woefully inadequate.

There are no words adequate enough to convey his sorrow for her loss, no amount of platitudes that can soften the blow. Her life will never be the same again, her husband is dead and the next step will be to bury him. What a prospect, what a world of misery he is bringing to this young woman's door!

Well, now you're going to have to think on your

feet...this appears to be it. And Lucas looks over at a quaint cottage with a flourish of flowers growing beside the front door.

Easing his tall, muscular frame out of the car, Lucas makes his way across the quiet street and knocks on the cottage's front door. Getting no answer he tries again, Lucas taking a step back to look up at the bedroom windows for signs of movement.

Maybe she's out back – could be hanging some washing out on a day like this.

But when he makes his way to the back of the cottage there is no sign of any activity.

"Mrs Linden," Lucas calls out and waits for an answer, but none is forthcoming. Frowning, he moves forward to peer in through the back door which has been left slightly open. Then he gasps in shock, a frisson of ice cold fear running down his spine and almost stopping his heart.

"Mrs Linden, is that you?" he asks, staring down at the bare toes that are just visible through the crack of the door. "Mrs Linden..." he shouts more persistently, "...can you hear me?"

No answer. More silence follows and Lucas has to force himself to act. Slowly pushing the door against the weight of the woman lying on the floor on the opposite side, Lucas steps into a scene that could have been taken from the grisliest of horror movies.

"Oh, Jesus!"

Dragging out his mobile phone, Lucas immediately calls for an ambulance. "Yes it is an emergency...," he tells the telephone operative, "...she's lying very still in a pool of blood but I can feel a faint pulse!"

Eyes swollen, every surface of bared skin battered and bruised, Lucas can't imagine what has happened to this poor young woman.

Don't die! Please don't die! I can't stand any more tragedy in just one day!

Lowering himself carefully to the floor, Lucas gently takes her hand and strokes it. "You're going to be ok," he tells her, bending close to her bloodied ear and sweeping the long auburn hair that has fallen across her face out of her eyes. "An ambulance is on the way and I'll be right with you all the time. Just hang on a little while longer then we'll get you to the hospital and they'll look after you. Just hang on...don't you dare give up!"

Minutes feel like hours as Lucas continues to talk to Dianna Linden, encouraging her to hold on, to listen to his voice and stay with him.

If there is a God Lucas can almost believe that he's having a laugh, playing some ghastly joke that he'll catch on to soon and be able to laugh at; once he wakes up from this crazy nightmare that is!

When the ambulance arrives the paramedic stabilises Dianna as quickly as he can then she is rushed to hospital with the sirens blaring.

Activity in the back of the ambulance is nonstop – fluids are given via a needle going into her arm, and temporary dressings applied to open wounds.

Looking down into her battered and bruised face, Lucas finds himself praying for Dianna's survival.

No one deserves this! To lose her husband and be attacked by some maniac all on the same day – this is some kind of perverse pantomime that the fates are playing out at her expense!

Pulling up outside of the ER, the ambulance men are met by medics pre-warned about the seriousness of Dianna Linden's condition. Things start to move faster than Lucas can keep up with and he stands back to watch the experts go to work.

He wants to go with her, wants to pour his strength into her to keep Dianna alive. When he tries to follow the trolley as it is wheeled away with Dianna on it, Lucas is forcefully stopped by a burley Charge-nurse.

"You can't do anything but get in the way of the doctors," the young man informs him kindly but firmly. "But you can be useful in providing all the information you have to this nurse," and a young woman in a neatly pressed uniform moves forward to make herself known.

"I'm Gill," she tells Lucas, and putting a hand on his arm gently guides him into a nearby office.

Answering the few questions that he can, Lucas feels useless and frustrated. What the hell is going on? How can this even be real? First Davey and now his wife...

The nurse seems to sense his turmoil and says, "So, you are not actually related...but you know Mrs Linden's husband?"

"Yes." Then Lucas scrubs at his haggard face with large trembling hands. "I'm his boss...or I was," he frowns sorrowfully, then begins to laugh almost hysterically at the insanity of it all. When he pulls himself together Lucas apologises to the nervous looking nurse and says, "He was killed in an accident at the quarry this morning. That's what I was doing at their cottage – I'd come to give her the bad news..."

Looking shocked, and then sad, Gill gets to her feet, "I'm going to get you a cup of hot sweet tea...I think you need it."

Left alone, Lucas tries to pull his thoughts together. This is not doing anyone any good. Get a bloody grip man!

But visions of Davey's lifeless body and Dianna's broken and bloodied form fill his mind's eye. Like snapshots being shoved in front of him, Lucas can see and actually smell the blood and death that he has experienced during this catastrophic morning.

When they'd finally recovered Davey's body from the cab of the overturned truck, a united gasp of realisation had gone up from the workforce gathered around, their last hope gone now.

Their faces will be forever ingrained in his memory; sorrow, distress and even regret, with just a touch of suspicion in some of their eyes.

He can imagine what they were thinking – was the truck maintained properly, had he cut corners to reduce costs, was Davey really up to the job or should someone more experienced and able to handle the monster have been at the wheel?

He will have to go over everything, answer all the questions that will be asked just to satisfy himself that all that should have been in place had been. Lucas needs to know that Davey was fully entitled to be driving the huge dumper truck and that none of his old drug habits had caused his death and endangered the lives of the men working alongside him.

"Here you go," Gill holds a mug of tea out to Lucas. "Just sip at it slowly; I didn't make it too hot so that you can drink it right away."

Doing as he's told, Lucas cups the mug between his

hands, grateful for the warmth. "I feel cold as ice," he mumbles between sipping the tea.

"Yes, I think the shock of what you've been through is taking its toll," Gill agrees knowingly.

"What a bloody day!"

"I can't imagine it could get any worse," Gill sympathises.

"Just don't let her die and I'll walk away happy," Lucas tips the mug of tea up and polishes off the last of it.

"Mrs Linden is in a very bad way...," Gill tells him guardedly, "...but you can rely on the fact that we're doing everything we can to stabilise her."

Lucas looks over at her quickly, latching on to the fact that the nurse seems to be aware of more information.

"Did you look in on her...?"

"Yes, just briefly," Gill admits reluctantly. "They've taken her to theatre — we'll know more about her condition when she comes out again."

"You mean 'if' she comes out again," Lucas shakes his head in despair.

Watching Lucas torment himself with imagined possibilities, Gill advises him to go home. "We'll call and let you know when Mrs Linden comes out of theatre," she assures him. "I've got your mobile number; you need to go home and get some rest. There really isn't anything more you can do here."

But Lucas shakes his head more firmly, "I promised her I wouldn't leave her alone. If I can't do anything else, at least I can keep my word."

The waiting room is crowded and the chaos that surrounds him goes unnoticed by Lucas. He is in his own tortured world, feeling responsible for the death of a young man in the early years of marriage and now sitting waiting to see if his wife will join him.

"Mr Forrester...?" a middle aged man tries to get Lucas' attention. "You're the gentleman that came in with Mrs Linden aren't you?"

Easing out of his introspective thoughts, Lucas nods up at the doctor.

"If you'd like to come with me I'll update you on Mrs Linden's condition."

"She's alive? She made it?" he gasps almost disbelievingly.

The doctor smiles, "I'm pleased to say that she did — though Mrs Linden isn't out of the woods yet. Far from it, in fact," the doctor frowns down at him, his kindly eyes surveying the man before him.

Standing, Lucas pumps the doctor's hand like it's a lifeline. "I'll pay all the costs for her to get the best care," he states excitedly. "She'll need a private room and access to any specialists you recommend to make sure that she pulls through this."

Guiding Lucas into the office he had been in earlier with the nurse, Dr Clayton takes a seat then looks at the man sat opposite him with open curiosity.

"Am I correct in thinking that you are not actually a relative of Mrs Linden?" Dr Clayton frowns speculatively over at Lucas.

"Is that going to be a problem?" Lucas asks, stiffening his spine, ready to take on the establishment.

"No, no, not at all," Dr Clayton assures him hastily. "But it does beg the question as to why you would put yourself to such expense?"

"I explained that to Gill, the nurse who took down all the details I could give her," Lucas states defensively. "Mrs Linden's husband was in my employ until this morning when he died in an accident while working at my quarry. I think that's good enough reason for wanting to take care of his wife...don't you?"

Raising a brow, Dr Clayton takes a breath to give himself time to think, then says, "In all my years I've seen any number of patients survive when the odds were heavily stacked against them...but I have to admit, Mrs Linden's case is something of a miracle."

"Her injuries are that bad?" Lucas asks, dreading the doctor's confirmation.

"Oh yes," Dr Clayton nods. "Her previous stays with us

were far less serious, but this time she was lucky to survive let alone keep the baby she is carrying."

"Baby..." Lucas can hardly take in the startling news.

Then his mind clicks into gear and his eyes become fierce, "Previous stays? What the hell does that mean?"

Looking a little uncomfortable the doctor has to make a decision about how much to tell this man. "As you are not a relative I'm bound by patient confidentiality as to how much of Mrs Linden's medical history I can tell you," he explains.

"Then just answer me this...," Lucas demands, his eyes not softening in the slightest, "...did her husband do this to her? Has he been beating on her on a regular basis?"

Hesitating only a moment, the doctor gives a sad nod of his head. "We haven't seen Mrs Linden for about 6 months, but prior to that she was in and out of casualty with various injuries that she could never satisfactorily explain away. Though she tried," the doctor shakes his head. "But that is a common reaction for women in Mrs Linden's situation. They not only make up stories about falls they've had, they also blame themselves for being 'stupid' or 'incompetent'. There are any number of derogatory terms that these women apply to themselves, no doubt having heard those descriptions from their husbands or partners over and over again."

"Jesus!" Standing up, Lucas has to pace off some of the mad that is eating him up. "If I'd known..."

"If you'd known you would probably have sacked the young man on principal and the beatings may have escalated as a result," Dr Clayton tells him.

"Well I'd have had to do something!" Lucas glares back at the kindly man who seems too accepting of the situation in Lucas' book.

"Apart from offering a shoulder and some well meaning advice about refuges that they can go to, there is very little that can be done to help until the women themselves decide to seek it out," Dr Clayton proclaims knowledgeably. "The cycle will not be broken until the woman decides that enough is enough – when she runs out of excuses for her partner's actions or finally stops believing them herself."

"Many women tell us that their partner doesn't mean to hurt them – if only they had done this right or that better then it would never have happened." Pursing his lips on a frustrated sigh, Dr Clayton pushes up from his chair, "We give them all the information we can; telephone numbers and the names of people here that they can contact when they decide they are ready – but we can't force them to leave. Only they can make that difficult decision."

Realising that the doctor is in an impossible situation, Lucas' anger subsides and he holds out his hand, "I don't envy you your job. I can't imagine what it feels like to discharge these women knowing that, in all likelihood, they'll come back with even worse injuries. It must be very frustrating."

"It can be...," Dr Clayton confirms with a rueful smile, "...but we have to take solace in the ones we manage to save. Not all of our abused ladies are discharged home – some decide that they can't face another day of it and are discharged into the care of a refuge. Those places have been the lifeline of many women - young and old, from upper class to working class, this kind of abuse knows no boundaries."

Nodding his understanding, Lucas follows the doctor out of the small office and back into the melee of the ER.

"If you'd like to follow me, I'll take you up to the ward for a very short visit with Mrs Linden."

Barely hearing the cacophony of crying babies, people demanding to be seen and others moaning in pain, Lucas can only think of Dianna.

How long has this been going on? Don't you have parents that you could have run to? Why...why would you stay even if you had no living relatives...surely there was someone you could have turned to, somewhere you could have gone?

Standing by her bedside, Lucas barely hears the explanations that the doctor is giving him. His mind and body seem to have gone into shock at the sight of Dianna's broken body – bandages, stitches, metal pins and a plaster cast to stabilise her broken bones...

"You need to sit down," Dr Clayton puts a little pressure on Lucas' shoulder and watches as he slumps onto the chair that he has placed at the back of his knees. "I realise that all of this can come as a shock, but we believe that Mrs Linden will make a full recovery – though the next 48 hours are critical."

Not taking his eyes from Dianna's brutalised face, Lucas nods his understanding. "You make sure that she has the best doctors and specialists to take care of her. I'll pay for everything...and don't leave her alone...I don't ever want her left alone. Is that clear?" Lucas tears his eyes away from Dianna for the instant it takes to show his hardened resolve and to see the doctor agree to his demand. "You take good care of her..." his voice has lowered to a reverent whisper as he very carefully takes Dianna's hand in his, "...it's about time someone showed you some kindness."

<u>CHAPTER TWO</u>

"Why are you putting yourself through this? You got her the best care there is and you spend half your life at that hospital," Hank states, bemused and concerned for his boss and life-long friend. "Now you want to take her into your home...I don't get it!"

"In many ways, neither do I," Lucas confesses with a frustrated frown. "I know I don't owe her anything — though Davey dying at work as he did does make me at least partially responsible for her situation."

"Fuck that!" Hank explodes. "Davey was high as a flaming kite when he drove that dumper truck over the edge and ended up dead at the bottom of the quarry — you couldn't have known he was going to do that...no one could!"

"I should have sacked him when I had the chance — maybe then he'd still be alive!"

"Don't give me that! If you'd 've sacked Davey, he would probably have killed himself with the drugs," Hank declares firmly. "Instead of which, you gave him 6 months off, with pay, to get himself straightened out. And he did get straight – I don't know what pushed his buttons that day...but I swear he wasn't using up till then!"

Heaving a heavy sigh, Lucas closes his eyes then looks across his desk at Hank. "I do. Dianna told me that that's when she told Davey he was going to be a dad."

Hank's jaw drops and his eyes go wide, "She was pregnant?!"

"She is pregnant," Lucas corrects. "Apart from the miracle of Dianna surviving her injuries, another miracle helped that baby to survive and it now seems to be flourishing."

A smile tugs at his lips as Lucas thinks of the moment when Dianna awoke and was told that her baby had survived. That look alone was worth all the hours of waiting for Dianna to come round. It was beautiful. She was beautiful...is beautiful...

"Well, that's good news for a change," Hank grins and picks up his mug of tea to drain it.

"Yes, exactly what I thought," Lucas agrees. "Come on, let's take a look at what's going on outside – the mechanics will be working on the damaged dumper truck."

The giant truck had been righted and towed to the top level of the quarry.

"These monsters don't damage easily," Gary Stephens, the mechanic, tells them when they reach the truck he's still working on. "The cab took a bashing, and the driver's side door'll want replacing, but the rest is just lumps and bumps that I'm working on bashing out."

"Any damage to the engine?" Lucas asks.

"Just needs a good tune-up...," Gary smiles. "She's beaten up some but, all in all, she's in relatively good nick!"

"Lucky for us," Hank chuckles softly. "We need her back in action if we're to meet our monthly target."

Scratching at his chin, Gary purses his lips while considering, "Well, I attached a couple of leads that had jostled loose – that's why you couldn't start the engine and drive her out of the quarry – and I already replaced the broken lights so...apart from waiting for the replacement door I ordered, I should be able to get her back in action by the end of the week. That soon enough?"

"Sounds good, Gary," Lucas smiles, then he and Hank head off back to the site office. "Ok, that's not as bad as I'd feared. We can take up the slack for one more week. Thank the gods it wasn't any worse!"

Feeling frightened and disoriented, Dianna awakes and thinks she is back in her own home with Davey. "No, Davey no...stop...please stop!"

The nurse looking after her quickly crosses the private room to console her. "It's alright, Dianna. You're alright," she repeats until her patient calms and wakens fully. "You're in the hospital...remember?"

Tears slide from her still swollen eyes. It's been two weeks since she'd been found broken and bleeding on her kitchen floor, but the nightmares still haunt her.

"He's gone. Davey's gone."

"I know, Dianna. But you need to focus on you for now; grieving for your husband will take time and energy that you need to get yourself well again."

"You don't think I should grieve for him," Dianna cries softly. "Just because he did this to me it doesn't mean that he didn't love me...because he did," she declares more firmly. "It was all my fault! If I hadn't gotten pregnant, if I hadn't burdened him with unnecessary worries...worries he couldn't cope with...he would never have done this. Davey was getting so much better-"

"Stop it!" Lucas demands from the doorway. Stepping further into the room, he crosses to Dianna's bedside and draws up a nearby chair.

This is crazy, Davey almost killed her and she takes

every opportunity to take it all on herself and exonerate him of any blame.

"You can't keep blaming yourself for Davey's actions, Dianna. He almost killed you...do you understand that?!"

Reaching out, Lucas gently takes Dianna's frail hands and feels like a heel for making her bottom lip tremble so badly. "I'm sure Davey did love you, but what he did to you was all down to him...not you."

Patiently, Lucas sits quietly watching the tears continue to slide from Dianna's blue eyes and can only hope that one day soon she will come to terms with the harsh reality.

Fuck it! Who made me judge and jury anyway. And what gives me the right to force my opinions on her. If Dianna wants to remember her husband in a certain way then maybe I should let her...just take a step back and let her keep her rose coloured memories...

But Lucas doesn't really think that will benefit Dianna in the long run. How will she move on with her life if she can't accept her past, the pain and humiliation that she suffered at the hands of a man who had a warped perspective where love was concerned?

Isn't that how this thing gets perpetuated? How a woman ends up getting involved with exactly the same sort of man again? If Dianna always sees the fault as being her own, and not the unacceptable behaviour of the man involved, how will she ever be able to discern the difference between a healthy relationship and an abusive one?

Hell, women shouldn't be put in that situation in the first place!

"Did you get a good night's sleep?" he asks quietly, watching as Dianna struggles to stem her tears.

Nodding carefully, still suffering with the most awful headaches, Dianna attempts a smile. "I must have been in a very deep sleep – I don't even remember dreaming," she murmurs tremulously.

"Good. That's good," Lucas smiles brightly, and is pleased to see Dianna's smile brighten in response. "I want you to consider an idea I've had, Dianna. I had a word with your Consultant and he agrees that, if you had proper home nursing care, you could be discharged at the end of this week," he tells her cautiously. Then adds, "But only if you consent to stay with me so that you have someone with you. They won't let you return home alone."

Shocked and bemused, Dianna can only stare at Lucas. Why on earth would you even consider doing that for me? I don't really know you, and I could never afford to pay for a private nurse... But Dianna can see that Lucas is sincere in his desire to take care of her, she just can't fathom why.

"Is this because you feel guilty about the way Davey died?" she frowns up at him. "Because if it is-"

"It isn't!" Lucas snaps, a little more sharply than he intended. "I mean...of course I feel bad that Davey died while working for me, but that isn't why I want to help you." Lucas lets out a long sigh and scrubs at his handsome face with two strong hands. "I just want to take care of you till you're well enough to look after yourself – is that such a bad thing?"

Nibbling nervously on the inside of her bottom lip, Dianna considers then shakes her head tentatively.

"I don't suppose so...I just don't know why you would put yourself to so much trouble and expense."

Letting out a rueful chuckle, Lucas smiles over at her and his grey eyes sparkle, "You're not the only one who thinks I'm crazy. My foreman thinks I've misplaced a few brain cells, too!"

Dianna manages a small laugh, but cringes when the cuts to her lips pull open and the nurse quickly wipes a drop of blood away.

"Let me apply some Vaseline...," the nurse suggests, "...it will help soften the scabs and make your lips less likely to bleed."

"Ok."

With gentle gloved fingers, the nurse applies the salve and smiles, "They're almost healed...just a couple of small scabs left. They'll no doubt fall off in the next few days," she reassures her patient.

Feeling suddenly self-conscious, Dianna takes her hand out of Lucas' and lifts it to cover her mouth.

"It doesn't matter...," he soothes, taking back her hand and holding it at her side, "...I saw you when you were beat to a pulp. Now you just look funny with all the colours your skin has turned."

The nurse chokes out a cough of disbelief and isn't surprised when Dianna rebukes him.

"Very gentlemanly, I don't think!"

"Well you do," Lucas insists, not holding back his laughter. "But now I can see how pretty you are beneath them."

Now Dianna looks flabbergasted! "Well...thank you...I think." *You are so weird! You go from insults to compliments in the blink of an eye. And you have such nice eyes...kind eyes...*

Her mind takes Dianna's thoughts in an unexpected direction, one where those eyes are smouldering and looking at her as no man ever has before. Her heart rate spikes and the monitor she's connected to begins to alarm.

"So, will you let me take you out of here and take care of you till you're back on your feet?" he asks, suddenly earnest, his laughter forgotten.

"What...? Oh...alright," she agrees, and struggles to pull her wayward thoughts back to the here and now. Her smile is shy and cautious so as not to break the wounds on her lips open again.

"That's a girl. Just a few more days and you'll be able to sit out in the garden and get some fresh air," Lucas smiles encouragingly. And I'll be able to take proper care of you, the way you should be cared for!

"Sounds like heaven," Dianna sighs. "But are you really sure you want to burden yourself with me - I could just wait until I'm well enough to go home?"

"Is that what you really want...to stay here for another two weeks?"

I can't wait to get out of this place. As lovely as the nurses are, I just want to go home. "No, not really. I just don't understand why-"

"Put all of that out of your mind," he tells her gently. "Just accept that I want nothing more than to help a fellow human being in her time of need and go with it."

"Alright...," she agrees, "...I'll just go with it."

CHAPTER THREE

For the umpteenth time, Lucas reminds his kindly housekeeper that they have two guests arriving today.

"Yes, Mr Forrester, the rooms are ready and the intercom has been fitted," a very patient Helen Layton tells him.

"But have you tried it out?" Lucas asks, and gets his answer when the housekeeper looks nonplussed.

"Ok, let's give it a try," he suggests, already leaving the lounge and heading up the large staircase.

"You take the nurse's room and I'll take Dianna's – I'll try alerting you and if it's working I want you to pick up," Lucas orders, then marches off to carry out his plan.

Pressing the 'call' button, Lucas hears the ringing tone and then hears Helen say, "It seems to be working just fine, should I do anything else?"

"Yes, just try doing it the other way – put the phone down and you call me," Lucas tells her, then frowns when he hears her chuckle before replacing the handset.

Sure enough his telephone rings and he answers it, "Good. Good. At least we know that Dianna will be able to call her nurse if she needs her in the night. Thank you, Helen."

Hearing the crunch of gravel on the drive, Lucas crosses to the front of the house to see who has just arrived.

"Here we go, Helen – the ambulance has just arrived," Lucas tells her as they meet up on the landing.

"Will you want me to greet the lady or should I go and prepare tea?" Helen asks politely.

"Greet first and then tea," Lucas calls over his shoulder as he rushes to open the large front doors.

"Mr Forrester...?" a neatly uniformed nurse greets him as he exits the house.

"That's me – are you Nurse Baxter?"

"I am indeed," she smiles, though her demeanour is still stern. "Mrs Linden will need to rest after her journey, but appears to be fine."

"Thank you, nurse," Lucas smiles delighted. "I'll help you to get Dianna inside."

But the nurse puts up a hand and says, "No need, Dr

Harvey accompanied me and will assist with the transfer."

Feeling a little put out, Lucas stands back as a far too handsome doctor around his own age assists Dianna out of the ambulance.

"That's great, Dianna. Just take it steady and move at your own pace," Dr Harvey advises.

Her progress is slow, but Dianna eventually makes it to her room and is delighted by its decor and furniture.

"This is wonderful," she smiles at Lucas. "You are so kind to allow me to stay here."

"Not at all...," Lucas smiles, feeling a little mollified by her delight, "...I want you to make yourself completely at home and feel free to explore the house and gardens when you are up to it."

Looking out of the French doors leading to a good sized balcony, Dianna's smile widens, "Oh the garden is beautiful, I should really enjoy sitting out for a while."

While Lucas looks happy to oblige her, the nurse is less enthusiastic. "Not just yet, Mrs Linden. You need rest and relaxation after your trip – if your observations are acceptable after your rest, it may be possible for you to venture out this afternoon."

Both Dianna and Lucas look crestfallen, and Helen has to stem a smile. "If you'd like a cup of tea I'm sure it wouldn't hurt for you to take it on the balcony," Helen observes, and gives the nurse a challenging look. "That way you can rest and get some fresh air at the same time."

Brightening instantly, Dianna and Lucas turn to the nurse who gives an indignant sniff, "I imagine that would be alright...as long as Mrs Linden is seated in a comfortable chair with a footstool and a blanket to keep the chill away."

Giving Helen an extra bright smile, Lucas thanks her, "Excellent idea, thank you. If you wouldn't mind asking Bill to come up, we'll have comfortable seating arranged by the time you have the tea made."

Giving the nurse a respectful, though somewhat self satisfied smile, Helen leaves the room.

Dr Harvey has been watching the little drama with interest, "Take a rest on the bed for now, Dianna; Nurse Baxter can get your observations done while we wait."

When Bill arrives he helps Lucas to carry a chaise longue from his mother's old bedroom out onto Dianna's balcony. "Thank you, Bill that should do very nicely!"

Dr Harvey looks up from Dianna's chart and gives a pleased nod, "Yes, very good. An hour in the fresh air will give you a nice boost. But no longer than that...," Dr Harvey smiles, "...we don't want you overdoing things on your first day."

By the time Helen comes back with a tray of tea and a plate of assorted biscuits, Dianna is settled on the chaise longue on the balcony with Lucas sitting on a chair nearby.

Putting the tea tray down on the small occasional table stood between them, Helen pours two cups and hands one to Dianna, "Would you like a biscuit with that? I baked them fresh this morning," she smiles encouragingly.

Choosing one, Dianna takes a bite and groans, "Oh my, these are wonderful. I can see I'm going to have to be careful, I could eat a plate of these all to myself," she chuckles happily.

"You're looking a lot better already," Dr Harvey smiles, coming onto the balcony after Helen leaves. "I believe your progress will be much quicker in these very pleasant surroundings."

"I think you're right...," Dianna returns his smile, "...though I'll be forever grateful for what you and the hospital have done for me."

"That's our job, and you have been a very pleasant patient to look after," Dr Harvey tells her, giving a small bow of his head.

Not sure why, Lucas feels extremely irritated by the doctor's too charming manner and Dianna's enthusiastic response to it.

"Won't the hospital be needing you to get back?" Lucas asks, his smile only marginally softer than a sneer.

Dianna lets out a shocked gasp but Dr Harvey just smiles and nods in agreement, "I do need to be leaving. But with your permission, I'd like to call in on you tomorrow?"

With her smile back in place, Dianna agrees, "That would be lovely, though I really don't think I need a doctor anymore."

"No, you're doing just fine," Dr Harvey agrees. "Though if your nurse feels it's necessary to call your GP go along with her; from what I know about Nurse Baxter's experience, you would do well to heed her advice," he tells her sagely. "So, as you no longer need me to be your doctor perhaps we could become friends?"

"Of course," Dianna chuckles. "But I can't keep calling you Dr Harvey if you visit as a friend."

"I'm Alex," he introduces himself, and holds out a hand to Dianna, who laughs and takes it willingly.

Christ almighty, can this man get any cheesier! Just get on your bike, Dr Alex, and don't bother coming back! "I'm sure Nurse Baxter will have things to do for Dianna tomorrow. She seems to be a very capable woman."

Instead of taking umbrage, as he's sure Lucas intended him to, Alex Harvey smiles and turns his attention to their host, "I couldn't agree more. But I'm sure even the formidable Nurse Baxter will allow Dianna a visitor or two." Turning his handsome smile back to Dianna, Alex continues, "There are one or two nurses who have mentioned that they would like to come and visit you when you feel up to it?"

"I can never thank them enough for all they've done for me – of course I would love them to visit," Dianna beams brightly.

"Good, then I'll bring one of them with me tomorrow," Alex tells her, satisfied that she will not be excluded from the world on her host's say so. You may be being protective in some misguided way, but I won't let you isolate Dianna, not for any reason.

"I'm sorry that you don't like Alex," Dianna tells a very broody looking Lucas after the doctor has gone. "I think he just wants to check up on me – make sure I'm behaving myself," she chuckles, hoping to lighten the strained mood.

And it seems to work. At least, Lucas turns to her and gives Dianna a brief smile before getting to his feet, "Then I'd better leave you to get some rest – I have work to be getting on with," he tells her, then leaves abruptly.

Damn it! What the hell is wrong with you, man – she's nothing to you, just a sick woman who needs a place to stay for a while.

Slamming into his home office, Lucas picks the phone up to speak to his foreman on site. When Hank picks up, Lucas is still in a bad mood, "Did that Parsons order get out on time?!" he demands without preamble.

Lifting a brow, and taking a calming breath before answering, Hank says, "Hello to you too, and yes...the Parsons order got out on time. Now tell me who crept up your arse and how long they'll be stayin'.'"

"Very funny," Lucas spits out, then lets go of a long sigh. "Just some jumped up doctor who seems to think Dianna needs him coming around checking up on her."

To Hank's surprise, he hears what sounds like jealously in his friend's voice. "You're not getting hung up on this woman are you?" he asks quietly. "She's only just become a widow-"

"I know that!" Lucas snaps out, cutting Hank off virtually at the knees. "And you're a fine one to be handing out advice on women – you can't keep one past a week!"

Instead of getting angry, Hank lets out a howl of laughter that only grates on Lucas' nerves, "That was a cheap shot. And I keep women for as long as I want to keep them. Any longer than a week and they think you're signing on for life!"

At that, Lucas can't help but give in to a laugh, "You

always have been scared of commitment."

"You can talk," Hank comes back smartly. "We're the same age, and I don't recollect you getting anywhere near to putting a ring on a woman's finger either!"

"Hmm...well, I can't deny that," Lucas reluctantly agrees. "But I'm not afraid of commitment; I just haven't found anyone I want to commit to."

Laughing easily, Hank tells Lucas that he's just splitting hairs, "You've had your share of beautiful women, I'm sure at least one of them would have made good wife material. What about Shelly, you two seemed good together?"

Yes, Shelly had been fun. No, she was more than fun...but it just wasn't enough... "I don't know what...but something was missing. It just didn't feel right...you know...?"

"Yeah, I know," Hank replies broodily; lately he's been feeling a strange kind of longing when he's been at his sister's house playing with her kids.

It's not like he wants to get married right away, but it would be nice to feel there is something 'more' on the horizon. In just a couple more years he will turn 40, same as Lucas, and he is beginning to feel like life is passing him by. But he doesn't allow himself to think too deeply about it.

"Anyway...," Lucas sighs, feeling on more of an even keel, "...I'll be in as usual tomorrow. Any problems you can get me here for the rest of today."

Nurse Baxter is as prompt as she is efficient, "It's time for a nap on the bed," she tells Dianna, lifting her fob watch to indicate that her hour to sit out on the balcony is up.

Enjoying the fresh air and the beautiful view, Dianna is reluctant to go in, but knows that the nurse is right. "I think I do need a nap..." and Dianna has to stifle a yawn as she gets awkwardly to her feet, "...I don't know why I'm so worn out, it isn't like I've been doing anything."

"Maybe not..." Nurse Baxter gives her a kindly smile as she puts a hand under Dianna's elbow to steady her, "...but even the trip here will have taken a lot out of you. And a good restorative nap will help get you back on your feet. But don't try to rush it; you've been through an awful lot."

Her sleep is fitful, her dreams filled with scenes from her last moments with Davey.

Please, Davey...please stop...

But Davey continues to shout and hit and blame her for making him do it. You just can't stop piling on the pressure. You just have to push it and push it until I can't take it any more...

And Dianna feels her face explode as his fist plunges into it one more time, "Noooo..." she screams and sits up abruptly in her bed, panting and holding a hand to her still aching cheek.

"It's alright, Mrs Linden...," Nurse Baxter puts a comforting hand across Dianna's shoulders and tries to calm her, "...it's just a dream. You're safe now, no one can harm you. It's all over."

When Lucas enters the room after hearing Dianna's scream from downstairs in his office, he is wide eyed and fearful.

"What the hell happened? Is she alright?" he asks breathing rapidly, his pulse pounding like a freight train.

"Mrs Linden had a bad dream," the nurse tells him while continuing to comfort Dianna. "Not unusual, considering the circumstances."

"I'm so sorry...," Dianna weeps, "...I'm so sorry."

"Will you stop apologising," Lucas tells her as he crosses the room to her bedside. "I was just worried that you'd fallen, or something."

"My head, it's thumping so hard..." Dianna gasps, laying back on her pillow and putting a hand to the left side of her forehead.

"I'll get you some pain relief," Nurse Baxter tells her and leaves Lucas to comfort Dianna.

Sitting on the side of her bed, Lucas leans in to put a hand to her forehead. "You haven't got a temperature but you're white and clammy."

"It's a reaction to the nightmare...," Nurse Baxter tells him as she returns to hand Dianna a couple of tablets and a glass of water, "...nothing to worry about."

"Thank you," Diana tries to smile up at the nurse but can't raise her eyes fully due to the pain in her head.

"Just rest a while, let the tablets get to work and then you can sit out of bed if you feel up to it," Nurse Baxter pronounces, like she's just offered a treat.

"Sounds good," Lucas smiles, laying a hand over Dianna's and stroking it gently. "You could lay on the chaise and watch TV if you like?"

"Yes...perhaps..." but Dianna has to close her eyes against the pain in her head. I hope these tablets start working soon...I don't think I've ever had a headache like this...it's unbearable.

Looking up at the nurse, Lucas' concern is clearly evident, "Are you sure she's alright? She looks white as snow and the pain is obviously bad."

"We'll give it half an hour – time for the meds to kick in and then we'll reassess," Nurse Baxter assures him.

Then she collects her equipment together and proceeds to do Dianna's observations, blood pressure, temperature, etc. and makes a note of them and her current condition in her file.

"I'll do your observations again in 15 minutes, just to check that they are remaining within acceptable limits," the nurse tells Dianna.

"Thank you," Dianna whispers, but doesn't open her eyes.

"You're all in," Lucas observes quietly. "Maybe sitting out on the balcony wasn't such a good idea. I probably encouraged you to overdo things and this is the result."

"No...," Dianna protests, finally opening her eyes to look up at him, "...you were very kind, and I loved sitting out – I've been cooped up in a small hospital room for weeks. I really think it was just the dream...just the reality of it all..."

More tears begin to slide down her pale cheeks and Lucas reaches over to brush them away.

"I'm sorry...about Davey," he clarifies when she looks confused. "I hate that he died at my quarry, but I'm not sorry that he can't do this to you ever again."

"No! No! Davey isn't the monster you think he is," Dianna protests vehemently, still using the present tense. "It was my fault – if I hadn't gotten pregnant...if I'd helped out more with the bills and the house..."

Standing abruptly, Lucas drops her hand and glares

down at Dianna, "When will you get it through your head that Davey almost killed you." And when he sees Dianna begin to shake her head he sees red, "Yes, Dianna – he fractured your skull, smashed your left cheekbone, broke 3 ribs...one of which punctured your lung and, just to round it off, he kicked you so hard while you were lying on your kitchen floor that he also managed to break your left leg!" Pushing his hands back through his hair, Lucas grips it in his hands and squeezes.

"I.I'm s.sorry," Dianna cringes back into her pillows, her eyes round with fear.

Nurse Baxter comes hurrying back into the room and glares at Lucas, "What on earth do you think you're doing, frightening Mrs Linden like this!" Crossing the room quickly, she sits on the side of Dianna's bed and takes her hand. "He won't hurt you, Mrs Linden, I wouldn't let him!" And she glares up at Lucas to reinforce her words.

"What?! What the hell are you talking about?!" Lucas gasps, his eyes wide and disbelieving.

Then he looks at Dianna and realises that he has indeed frightened her. "Dianna...I would never...I didn't mean... Bloody hell!" And Lucas strides from the room, the door closing behind him with a resolute click.

"There now, you just relax..." the nurse tells Dianna, "...I'll sit beside you for a moment then I'll take your observations again. Though they're bound to be elevated now," she tuts testily.

In his office, Lucas is berating himself loudly.

"You idiot! The woman just got out of the hospital after a beating from a man and you go off on one and scare the poor woman half to death! Brilliant, Lucas. Really well done!"

CHAPTER FOUR

All the following week, Lucas spends long hours at the quarry and avoids Dianna as much as good manners will allow.

He phones the nurse during the day to check up on Dianna and he puts his head in to say hello when he gets home from work, but Lucas doesn't linger.

Sitting out on her balcony, Dianna watches Lucas as he strides through the garden and out of sight.

Oh dear, I really have upset him. And Lucas is so kind, I should have known he would never have struck me...but...for just a moment... Oh you stupid woman!

Watching for his return, Dianna remembers her arrival at the house, how attentive Lucas had been.

He seemed so pleased to see me again, welcoming me with his brightest smile.

Remembering that smile makes Dianna sad, she misses the way they were and determines to set things right again.

"I've brought you some breakfast, Dianna," Helen announces from the bedroom, and watches as Dianna wheels herself from the balcony in the wheelchair that Alex Harvey had brought for her. "Looks like you're getting good with that."

Smiling sadly, Dianna looks at her plastered leg elevated in front of her and then up at Helen, "I feel clunky and awkward, but at least I can move around independently."

Adjusting the table so that Dianna can get to her breakfast, Helen arranges the teapot and cup so that she can pour herself a drink when she's ready.

"Thank you, Helen."

Dianna sounds sad and wistful to Helen's ears and she determines to find out why. "Is there something wrong, Dianna?"

Pushing the cereals around in her bowl, Dianna frowns down into them wondering what she can say. "I've upset Lucas and I don't know how to put things right," she admits quietly.

"Upset how...?"

Rubbing a hand over her eyes to stop the tears that

she is so sick of crying, Dianna looks up at Helen and lets it all out. "I can't even remember how it started, but I seemed to be defending Davey, telling Lucas that he wasn't a monster and that I had pushed him way too far when I already knew that he was under a great deal of pressure," Dianna recounts quickly, a hand to her stomach as she remembers that it was the prospect of becoming a dad that had tipped Davey over the edge.

"And it was my fault," Dianna insists. "But that's when Lucas got mad..." her voice quietens to little more than a whisper, "...and it frightened me. I know Lucas would never hit me..." she looks up at Helen with desperate blue eyes, "...but at that moment, and right after the hellish dream I'd just woken from..."

"I get the picture," Helen assures her, and draws up a chair to sit by Dianna. "And I'm glad to hear that you sensed that much about Lucas – he wouldn't harm a fly if he could avoid it. Apart from my husband, Bill, I've never met a man more willing to put himself out to help someone in need. He's a good man."

"I know. And I'm really sorry that I've upset him...but what can I do to put things right when he doesn't stay long enough for me to apologise?"

"Hmm." Helen gives the matter some thought then smiles, "Well, you can eat all that breakfast for starters.

Then I'll get Bill to help us down the stairs and bring your wheelchair down and you can go out in the garden and talk to Lucas yourself," Helen finishes on a satisfied smile.

Coughing on her cereal, Dianna looks panic stricken, "Really? You think that's a good idea?"

"I do..." Helen stands and moves to the door, "...and if I know Lucas half as well as I think I do, he'll be only too glad to put it all behind you both. He's been like a bear with a sore head all week," Helen moans as she descends the stairs.

Oh Lord! I don't know if I'm brave enough to do this. And looking into her cereals and milk, Dianna tries hard to eat them but has completely lost her appetite.

When Helen returns with Bill, Nurse Baxter is standing with her arms folded at Dianna's side. "What's this I hear about a trip into the garden? It could be extremely dangerous to take Mrs Linden down those stairs while she is in such a weakened state and with her cast still in place!"

"Which is why I brought my husband with me," Helen brushes the nurse's objections aside. "Between us we'll get Dianna safely down the stairs and let her do as she pleases – and if that is taking a turn about the garden in her wheelchair then good for her!"

With the two iron willed women glaring at each other,

Bill moves forward to intervene. "No need for cross words," he sooths firmly, then moves to Dianna. "If you'll permit me, I'd be happy to carry you down the stairs – you're only a little thing and it would be no trouble?"

Looking from Helen to Nurse Baxter, Dianna nods with relief, "That would be fine...thank you, Bill." And winding her arms around his neck she feels herself lifted by two very strong arms.

"I'll come back for the wheelchair," he tells the two women who look fit to burst with indignation, then moves quickly out to the landing and down the stairs. "There now, you just sit for a minute and I'll get your wheelchair," Bill tells Dianna after setting her down in the lounge.

"Bill..." Dianna whispers, "...thank you so much."

Giving her an understanding grin, Bill makes his way back up to Dianna's bedroom and passes his wife stomping down the stairs with a look of thunder on her face.

"I can't wait till that bloody woman is gone," Helen tells no one in particular. "I could look after Dianna just as well as she can!"

A few minutes later and Dianna is wheeling herself into the garden in search of Lucas. When she spots him deadheading some flowers, Dianna hesitates in the shadows.

The sun is brilliant in a clear blue sky and she can hear happy birds singing for the glory of it. Barely a whisper of wind stirs the leaves and petals, just enough for Dianna to smell the scents of the beauty surrounding her.

Even more spectacular than I could see from my window. It's more real and much more beautiful from this perspective. And so is Lucas!

I shouldn't be thinking like this, I don't want to be attracted to him...but...

Reaching high to clip a climbing rose over a lattice arch has Lucas' muscles straining in a way that has Dianna sighing and swallowing hard. His thighs are covered in casual denim, and it does nothing to hide the sexy contours of a body made to please and pleasure a woman.

Moving forward cautiously, Dianna tries to push down the images of Lucas naked in her bed, of her hands ranging over the dips and hollows of his taught body before he takes her up to the highs of a heaven she can only imagine.

"Hello, Lucas," she smiles shyly, hoping that he won't turn and walk away.

"Dianna," he gasps in surprise. "How did you get out here?"

"Bill carried me down then got my wheelchair," she

explains, and draws her bottom lip in nervously.

"I don't see Nurse Baxter – did she approve this little outing?" he asks, looking behind Dianna for the formidable nurse.

"Err..."

"That would be a no then," Lucas grins suddenly, and Dianna feels herself floating on air, so happy to see his handsome face alight again.

"Actually, Nurse Baxter and Helen had a bit of a standoff – but I don't know who won as Bill took me downstairs out of the way," Dianna tells him in a conspiratorial whisper.

"Good man!" Lucas declares heartily. "Well, come and enjoy the garden now that you've escaped your tower and the wicked witch," he invites with his brightest smile.

Dianna doesn't move, but sits looking up at Lucas with troubled eyes.

"What?" he asks eventually.

"I...Lucas...I need to apologise," she begins, but Lucas just waves it away.

"No need. I was an unthinking clod who should have known better," he declares, his lovely smile still in place. "Now come and enjoy the garden while you can. I don't imagine Nurse Baxter will let you out for long."

"She isn't so bad," Dianna smiles as she wheels herself

forward. "In fact, she can be quite chatty and happy when-" Catching herself, Dianna stops mid-sentence and looks guiltily up at Lucas.

"When things are going her way...?" Lucas finishes for her, and they both chuckle at the thought. "I could ask for another nurse if she doesn't suit you," he offers seriously.

"No. Oh no, she really is a treasure," Dianna exclaims quickly. "You just have to know how to take her – she doesn't mean any harm."

"Well...if you're really sure...?"

"I am. Nurse Baxter is an excellent nurse and looks after me very well. Now, I'd love to see your garden," Dianna smiles and moves further along the flower lined pathway.

"I have a gardener, but I enjoy pitching in when time allows," Lucas declares proudly. "I'm just deadheading these roses – they flower more and for longer if you get rid of the ones that have gone over."

"My mother used to love gardening," Dianna recalls. "My dad enjoyed sitting in a well-kept garden but, other than mowing the lawn, he didn't actually like gardening." Then Dianna giggles happily, "Actually, I doubt my dad would have cut the grass if mum hadn't bent his ears on a regular basis. She liked her garden to look really spick-and-span."

Flicking an eyebrow up, Lucas looks around the large garden and smiles, "Hmm, I'm on your mother's side. I like a neat garden, but I'm not a stickler. And anyway, Jimmy is stickler enough for both of us," he chuckles deeply.

"Is Jimmy your gardener?" Dianna smiles, feeling entirely at ease with Lucas now.

"He is, and a lot else besides," he tells her, continuing to remove any dead roses. "He's a very handy man to have around – and I suppose that's where the name 'handyman' comes from."

When Helen appears with a tray of chilled orange juice and a plate of her homemade biscuits she is gratified to see Dianna's eyes light up and her smile widen. "I thought you might enjoy these," she tells them as she sets the tray down on a nearby garden table.

Dianna wheels herself across and Lucas takes a seat nearby. "Just what I need," he sighs after taking a good drink. "It's hot out here today – maybe we should get you a hat?" Lucas suggests, narrowing his eyes to assess Dianna.

"No need, I have your medications, Mrs Linden," Nurse Baxter tells her sternly. "While I advocate taking in some fresh air, I also caution sitting out in this heat without sensible precautions – thus I brought you a hat and some sun cream, both supplied by Mrs Layton."

And to Dianna's surprise the two women actually exchange smiles.

Well, whatever they said to each other after Bill took me down stairs must have worked a miracle – they actually seem...well...friendly!

After giving Dianna her tablets and watching her take them, Nurse Baxter lifts her fob watch and then looks back at her patient, "Another half hour and then a rest on the bed for a while, I think. You'll tire easily at first – best to take it slow and easy."

Nodding obediently, Dianna smiles up at Nurse Baxter and offers her a seat. "Why don't you sit out with us for a while?"

"That's a good idea..." Helen agrees, "...I'll fetch another glass and pour you some chilled juice, Gillian."

"Well...alright, thank you, Helen," Nurse Gillian Baxter smiles.

Dianna and Luke can only look at each other in amazement, but decide to keep quiet.

"I spoke to Dr Harvey just now..." Nurse Baxter informs Dianna, "...and he said he would call round this afternoon, if that is alright with you? If not, I'm to let him know."

"He's so kind; Alex is run off his feet but still finds time to fit me into his busy schedule," Dianna enthuses quietly.

"A regular saint," Lucas murmurs, and doesn't care who hears him.

Looking startled at Lucas, Dianna isn't sure what to say. "I...well...maybe we should ask Lucas if it's alright?" Smiling hesitantly, Dianna watches his brows draw together in an annoyed frown.

"Sure, why not," he replies, then goes back to working on the nearby roses, deadheading them with a little more relish.

Drawing in her bottom lip, Dianna worries that she is outstaying her welcome. But you're the one who insisted I come here! Now you get annoyed when someone wants to visit with me – what am I supposed to think?!

As soon as Nurse Baxter has finished her orange juice Dianna suggests they go in, her joy at sitting out in the garden having dulled.

"Yes, good idea, you're looking a little peaky," Nurse Baxter agrees, scrutinising Dianna's face and sagging shoulders with professional concern.

Instead of fighting for her independence and insisting on wheeling herself back into the house, Dianna allows the nurse to take charge.

Not even thinking about how Nurse Baxter is going to get her back upstairs, Dianna is surprised to find herself wheeled through to the kitchen.

"Helen, I'm sorry to bother you when you are clearly busy...but do you think Bill could-"

Not giving the nurse time to finish her request, Helen waves her concerns aside and puts her head out of the window and calls for her husband. "Bill's on his way," she turns back to them and smiles. "He won't mind taking you back up," Helen tells them happily. Then she narrows her eyes at Dianna, "And none too soon by the looks of you, Dianna. Are you feeling alright?"

Trying to pull her smile back into place, Dianna only finds herself feeling desperately sad. Then, to her horror, tears she hadn't even realised had gathered begin to fall down her pale face.

"Dianna...," Helen gasps and quickly crosses to the young woman's side, "...whatever's wrong?"

"I don't know...," Dianna whimpers, her tears not slowing down, "...I just feel...sad."

"I think Dianna is a little tired after her exertions," Nurse Baxter puts in, and when Bill walks in the door she gives him a welcoming smile.

"Now then, someone need a lift?" he jokes, ignoring Dianna's obvious tears and lifting her swiftly into his strong arms. "We'll soon have you resting nice and peaceful like, back in your room," he smiles kindly as he carries her with seemingly little effort up the wide staircase.

Feeling herself laid gently on her bed, Dianna snuggles into the blanket that someone has kindly drawn over her. Moments later she is fast asleep and dreaming of Davey.

In her dream, Davey is happy to hear the news that they are expecting their first child. He wraps her in his arms then lifts her off her feet, doing an exuberant twirl.

He is so happy, so thrilled to hear he's going to be a dad; Davey can't wait to tell the guys at work.

"Have you thought of any names?" he asks, his eyes wide with wonder. "Is it a boy or a girl?"

Giggling with joy, Dianna wraps her arms around her husband's waist and says, "We won't know if it's a boy or a girl until the 20 week scan, so no, I haven't thought about names yet."

Davey is his old self, the young caring man that she had met in their senior years at school.

But when Dianna awakes she has to come to terms with his loss all over again and renewed tears fall from her still closed eyes to soak into her pillow.

"Why are you so sad?" Lucas asks from his chair at her bedside, his voice gentle and warm. "Are you unhappy here?"

Not sure whether or not to feign still being asleep, Dianna at first doesn't answer.

"Well?" Lucas persists, not fooled at all.

"I'm perfectly happy," she lies, mutinously keeping her eyes tight shut.

"So you always cry when you're happy..." Lucas observes sarcastically, "...even in your sleep, it seems."

"I...you...why are you here? This is my bedroom and you shouldn't be in it," Dianna states ungraciously.

His instant laughter has her eyes flying open to stare at Lucas, "Well at least you haven't lost all your spirit, though it's taken long enough to surface."

"Oh!" she snaps in frustration, then childishly pulls the cover over her head to block him out.

That makes Lucas laugh even more, "Oh no you don't," and he pulls the blanket right off the bed in a sudden move that Dianna hadn't been expecting. "When I argue with someone I like to look them in the eyes," he grins into her stunned face.

"And who says I want to argue," she snaps back, flipping onto her other side and resolutely showing him her back.

"I do. And if it's the only way to get you to open up, I'm more than willing to oblige," he states airily.

Struggling to sit up, Dianna turns a red hot glare on Lucas that should have fried the flesh off his bones. "You think you know everything. Well you don't!"

Not phased at all, Lucas merely lifts a brow and says,

"Then why don't you enlighten me...I'm all ears?"

Narrowing her eyes, her temper building, Dianna gives it to him right from her twisted gut, "I didn't ask you to bring me here, you asked me. Now you get all bent out of shape when a kind person asks if they can visit me. Alex makes me feel like a human being again by taking the time to actually care that I exist!"

"And I don't?!" Lucas frowns, his annoyance growing despite his best efforts to rein it in.

"I didn't say that! Stop putting words in my mouth," she snaps, her voice growing louder with her rising anger.

Downstairs in the kitchen, Nurse Baxter is having a cup of tea with Helen. "Maybe I should go up..."

"No, it's alright, Lucas is just trying to ease the floodgates open," Helen assures her. "It's way past time."

"Well if you didn't say it outright, you certainly implied it," Lucas throws back at Dianna. "And I do care. Why do you think I wanted you to come and stay here – and don't you dare say it was some kind of guilt reflex!"

"There you go again, putting entirely the wrong words in my mouth," Dianna huffs, both hands balled on her hips. "If you want to take care of both sides of the conversation then go and argue with yourself somewhere else!"

Getting swiftly to his feet, Lucas towers over her and

watches as she just as quickly covers her head with her hands and curls up on the bed as best her plastered leg will allow.

Just as shocked as the first time she'd cringed away from him, Lucas sucks in a breath and stands stock still.

"Dianna...I'm sorry...I didn't mean to frighten you," he tells her gently, his temper instantly disappearing. Lowering himself onto the bed he waits for Dianna to relax. When her hands move down to cover her mortified face, he gently strokes her long auburn hair.

He can feel the tremble that is still shivering through her and feels ashamed of his actions. "I will never hurt you, Dianna. I never could. I only want to take care of you."

"But you were angry..." she mumbles, her body slowly relaxing into the bed.

"You drive me crazy," he admits, chuckling softly, his hand still soothing away her fear and gentling her like a skittish colt. "When you were outside with me in the garden, you gradually came out of your shell and we shared a few pleasant moments. But you don't talk to me, Dianna...not really."

"I don't know what you want me to say," she whispers, her lie not even slightly convincing.

"Well...I suppose you could start by telling me what

happened on the morning I found you," Lucas encourages carefully. "You said that you told Davey about the baby and that that set him off, but I want to hear all of it, right from the start of your day."

CHAPTER FIVE

"Davey never meant to hurt me," Dianna begins, still lying on the bed, her face averted. "The morning started out so well...we were both smiling and chatting and I was bursting with the knowledge that I was pregnant."

When she falls silent, Lucas gives her a verbal nudge, "And..."

"And I was nervous," Dianna admits, not realising that she had been until now. "I don't really know why, I just couldn't seem to find the words... But Davey seemed to be so happy; happier than he's been in a long time," she admits. "And I think that was down to you and especially Hank."

Frowning, Lucas has to ask, "What makes you say that?"

Pulling herself up into a sitting position, Dianna smiles over at Lucas and his heart lifts to see it.

"You made him get help for his drug problem...and Hank took the time to go with him to his meetings and make sure that he was sticking to the programme," she tells him, her smile widening and actually putting a twinkle in her blue eyes.

"He was a good worker...," Lucas coughs to cover his embarrassment, "...and no boss worth his salt will turn his back on a good worker."

"You paid his wages even when he was off," Dianna reminds him, loving the way this big strong man can look so uncomfortable at being thanked for his kindness.

Shifting his position, Lucas moves back to sit on the chair. "Well, there we go...but you haven't finished your story," he reminds her, changing the subject adroitly.

"Hmm, well...I made Davey a cooked breakfast and he seemed pleased. Then he started getting ready for work and he kissed me, just before he turned to pull on his jacket." Again, she falls silent, only this time Lucas doesn't interrupt her thoughts, but waits patiently.

"At that moment, I know that Davey loved me," she whispers, her blue eyes looking far away at the memory. "He was so gentle...," and her hand lifts to lay against her cheek the way his hand had done that morning, "...so very loving. And then I spoiled it all by blurting out my news, stupidly thinking that he would be happy to hear it."

"But he wasn't...?" Lucas asks when Dianna again falls silent.

"No...he wasn't." Her eyes close as her heart twists with remembering. "It was like someone else had stepped into his body – the change was so quick and so profound. The love was gone, the gentleness vanished, and he was suddenly shaking me until my teeth rattled in my head." Her head was shaking now, her mind finding it difficult to accept the reality of what Davey had done to her.

"Finish it, Dianna," Lucas urges quietly but firmly.

"He...he was shouting...asking me why...why I was so hell bent on torturing him." A trembling hand moves to rub over her eyes, but it can't erase the awful memory. "I was so frightened I couldn't speak, and that seemed to make him even angrier." Swallowing hard, Dianna ignores her shame and forces herself to continue. "That's when he started to hit me. I don't remember how many times his fist pummelled my face, my body, the pain was too excruciating to think through. And eventually I just remember thinking that this was it, this time I was going to die."

Again Lucas waits, but this time he isn't encouraging her to go on because he is having trouble dealing with the images she has just put in his head.

How can any man do that! And to a woman he

professes to love! Was that his intention...to kill her? Was he so determined to get rid of the baby that he would have gotten rid of Dianna too? Bloody Hell!

"I can see your disgust...," she tells him with a sigh, "...it's written all over your face." And when Lucas looks up at her, Dianna is certain of what she must do next. "I'll ask Helen to call a taxi. It won't take me long to pack what few belongings I have."

Her voice is sad and her shoulders have slumped, resigned to the fact that her story has revolted him. And why not? He must think I'm pathetic...probably too polite to say so, but he thinks it nevertheless. He's lost any respect he might have had for me. I'm just not worth it...

"What the hell are you talking about?" Lucas asks when he realises what Dianna has just said.

"It's alright, you don't need to pretend. I can be out of here in a heartbeat, but I will need a taxi," she tells him forlornly.

"There will be no bloody taxi," Lucas states firmly, then softens his voice when he remembers to whom he is speaking. "Sorry, sorry, I didn't mean to shout. But what's all this rubbish about you needing a taxi — why on earth would you think I'd want you to leave?"

Seeing the sincerity in his eyes, Dianna realises that perhaps she's misread the situation, but is too unsure of herself to believe it. "I...I realise that I'm not the person you believed me to be. I mean, I should have been more honest with you..."

"Not the..." Lucas is totally confused now. But as he stares down at Dianna it suddenly becomes clear. "You think I'm disgusted by what you just told me?" he asks, incredulous. "Well, you're right, I am disgusted..." he huffs, "...but not with you. I'm disgusted that any man thinks he has the right to hurt a woman like that. Any woman," Lucas affirms sternly. "And yes, the fact that Davey hurt his wife, a woman who loved and stuck by him through thick and thin, is repugnant to me. It would be repugnant to most right thinking men!"

Dianna feels so relieved that a stream of tears falls down her pale cheeks and into her lap.

"Here now, stop that," Lucas rebukes her gently, and moves to sit beside her on the bed again. Putting an arm across her shoulders, he pulls her to him and holds her until the tears stop falling.

"I can never thank you enough," Dianna sniffs, her bottom lip trembling pathetically.

"I don't need your thanks," Lucas smiles, looking down into eyes still pooling with unshed tears. "All I want is to see that woman I caught a glimpse of when we were arguing. She had spirit, a sense of self that was worth standing up for. And anyway…" Lucas puts a gentle finger under Dianna's chin and smiles impishly, "…I enjoy a good argument. I find it clears the air and stimulates the mind."

At that, Dianna's lips pull into a shy smile. "I used to like that too. Before…when I was younger," she qualifies stiltedly. "My parents used to call me 'the hurricane'; apparently my temper was quick and stormy, but blew out just as quickly."

"Where are your parents, Dianna?"

"Oh, they moved to a warden controlled flat in Derbyshire. Mum couldn't keep up with the house and garden anymore, and Dad has needed more looking after since his stroke," Dianna smiles ruefully.

"So you don't get to see them?" he asks, watching Dianna intently.

"Well…no…but I don't drive and I couldn't pester Davey to keep taking me," she adds quickly. "He had enough to do with work, it wouldn't have been fair."

For a moment, Lucas just considers then asks, "They don't know that he beat you, do they?"

Gasping at his insight, Dianna pulls away, "It was our business. We were working things out, and I didn't want them getting the wrong idea."

Feeling himself stiffen again, Lucas gets to his feet, but slowly this time. Then he takes a walk around the room, trying to shove down the anger that now wants to explode.

"And what wrong idea would that be?" he asks, his voice dangerously low and as frightening to Dianna as if he had shouted.

"I don't know," she murmurs pathetically, not wanting to think too deeply about it.

"Really?! Might it be that they would have thought that Davey was a cowardly son-of-a-bitch who couldn't keep his fists off their daughter?" he muses scathingly. "Or were you worried that they might think less of you because you allowed it to go on? Either way, it would have meant you facing up to the truth – Davey was a lousy husband who didn't know the meaning of love and had no business being with you!"

All thought of herself vanished, along with her timid demeanour. "Don't you dare stand there casting aspersions on my marriage. You don't know what Davey was really like, any more than you know what I'm really like!" Now Dianna is standing stiff and tall, hands balled on both hips and her cheeks red with growing temper. "You have no right to stand in judgement of us!"

"No right! Damn it, Dianna, you can't hide the truth from me, I'm the one who found your broken body with just a breath of life left in it," Lucas rages as quietly as an angry man can. Taking a step towards her, Lucas puts a hand on both her shoulders and gives Dianna a gentle shake. "He was never good enough for you. Davey died because he couldn't face what he'd done."

As Dianna stares up at him, her anger replaced by sadness, her head begins to shake in denial of something that her heart has already begun to acknowledge.

He can't bear it. Her anger was better than the well of sadness that Lucas is now looking into. And before he knows what he's doing Dianna is in his arms and his lips are on hers.

The kiss is not gentle, neither one knows what is happening to them but it feels so right. All their pent up emotions pour into each other, their hands seeking and holding, their minds spinning onto a plane where reality doesn't exist.

His muscled body is plastered to Dianna's feminine curves and responds instantly.

Christ, you drive me crazy. I must be crazy...I want you. I need you. I...

Breaking away, Dianna wipes the back of her hand across her swollen lips and just stares up at Lucas, her breathing laboured, then takes another step back as his hand comes up.

Her world has shifted on its axis, and Dianna has

experienced a depth of passion that is difficult to deal with now that the reality of the situation is making itself known. Far from being afraid of Lucas, Dianna is afraid of herself, of her response to his mouth on hers, his hands exploring and moulding her body until her mind was screaming for...for...

"Oh hell, Dianna...I didn't mean...I'm so sorry..."

And when he makes to step towards her Dianna takes yet another step back. "Please don't," she begs softly. I don't know that I could stop you if you take me in your arms again. I'm a shameful, hateful woman for wanting you like this. My husband is barely cold in his grave and I'm behaving like a slut. Perhaps Davey was right about me all along...

"Please, don't look like that..." Lucas pleads as he watches her emotions play out on her tragic face, "...it was totally my fault. I just lost it. I had no right to kiss you, and I promise absolutely, it will never happen again."

Watching her silently nod in agreement, Lucas turns and walks out of the room before he does something they might both regret.

By the time Alex Harvey arrives, Dianna has calmed herself and is ready for company.

At least I know I'm safe with Alex. He's such a sweet man, and so considerate.

"How are you doing? You must be dying to get that cast off," Alex chuckles as Dianna hobbles across the bedroom to greet him.

"You are so right. The itching is driving me mad," Dianna grimaces. "Will it have to be on much longer?"

He isn't surprised that Dianna can't remember everything that was explained to her before she was discharged from hospital. Most people are overwhelmed by it all and often phone up to ask questions, once they've settled back at home.

"You've got one more week," Alex grins charmingly. "I could probably pick you up and take you if you'd like?"

"Won't you be working?"

"No. I checked your appointment before I left off yesterday; it's next Wednesday afternoon at 2.30. It's my day off then anyway," Alex shrugs dismissing her worries.

"You have a day off and you're willing to spend part of it taking me to hospital - that sounds...so sweet," she eventually smiles.

"Ok, that's sorted. Now, what would you like to do today," Alex asks jovially. "It isn't as warm as it was this morning, but it's warm enough to go to a park if you put a coat on."

For a moment, Dianna stops to think, then decides to ask his help with something she has only just realised she wants to do.

"Actually, Alex, there is somewhere I'd like to go," Dianna begins tentatively.

"Ok, name it and we'll be on our way."

"Well, it isn't a park, it's a cemetery," she finishes hesitantly.

For a moment Alex is taken aback, and then he nods and smiles with understanding. "Your husband. You haven't been to visit his grave yet?"

"No. Lucas has already done so much for me; I didn't want to put him to any more trouble."

Looking at her more carefully, Alex can see a few signs of stress. "Is everything alright? Are you still happy to stay here?"

Realising that her doubts had shown on her face, Dianna rallies to put the notion out of Alex's head. "Everything's fine. I'm being looked after like a princess. But I would like to visit Davey's grave. It's like he just disappeared from my life – I need to make his death real. If you understand me..."

"Of course," Alex tells her, his handsome face a picture of sympathy. "We'll go at once, and then I'll take you somewhere nice for lunch."

"Actually...I'm really sorry...but I've already eaten," Dianna admits feeling guilty.

"Oh. Well, not to worry. We can buy some bread and

feed the ducks after our visit to the cemetery," Alex tells her obligingly.

"You are so kind. I don't know why you even bother with me. I'm sure you don't have time to visit all your former patients," Dianna observes with a smile.

"I'm concerned for you, Dianna," Alex tells her sincerely. "You've had an extremely rough time of it, and I just want to make life a little better for you."

If she hadn't already got her head full of worries about Lucas, Dianna might have thought more about the sentiment that Alex was expressing.

But as it is, she doesn't give it another thought and sees his concern as an act of kindness by a dear friend.

"Your visits brighten my day," Dianna smiles happily. "Let's get off and enjoy the afternoon."

From an upstairs window, Lucas stands watching the two of them leave. Bill puts the wheelchair in Alex's car boot and wishes them a good trip. Dianna has her hand through Alex's arm, and with his other hand at the small of her back he slowly guides her to his car.

For a moment Dianna hesitates, feeling someone's eyes boring into her she turns and looks up, but there is no one there.

CHAPTER SIX

All week Lucas has wrestled with his feelings; pushing them aside, working so hard that he barely has time to think.

But Dianna is there no matter what he does. And so is Alex Harvey.

Pacing in his office, Lucas tries to read the invoice that Hank has given him, but his mind is in turmoil.

"It's unethical to get involved with a patient!" Lucas suddenly expounds, turning to look at his foreman. "Harvey could get struck off, couldn't he?" Lucas adds hopefully.

"What the...?" Hank is confused, the sudden change in conversation plucked right out of the blue. "Who the hell is Harvey?"

"Harvey! Alex Harvey..." Lucas frowns at Hank as

though he suspects him of being deliberately obtuse, "...Dianna's doctor. He's picking her up from the house and taking her to get the cast off her leg today!"

Raising a brow, Hank regards his friend with open curiosity. "Not like you to let another man move in on a woman you're interested in."

"I'm not-" Stopping short of making an instinctive denial, Lucas gives the side of his desk a thunderous kick. "Oh fuck it! Yes, damn it, I am interested in her. I'm more than just interested in her! But I'm trying to keep my distance and it's driving me crazy. Especially knowing that smarmy bastard, Doctor Alex Harvey, is hanging around in the background!"

Lucas paces the floor of their office with suppressed emotions churning him up inside. It's been like hell on earth staying away from Dianna; afraid to be near her in case his feelings for her get out of hand again. It had been wonderful to hold her, to taste Dianna until his mind had been drugged senseless by her. He doesn't trust himself to be in the same room as a woman who can make his basic instincts go into overdrive that way.

"Sounds to me like it's time to stop prevaricating and go get your woman," Hank grins, then chuckles deeply when Lucas's frown deepens. "Davey's gone — dead and buried. You carry on trying to do the honourable thing and someone else is going to beat you to the post. Get the fuck out of here and take her to the hospital yourself!"

Looking at his watch, Lucas realises that he probably has time to get home and take Dianna before Harvey arrives. "Any problems, you know where I'll be," he grins, swiping car keys off the desk before he leaves.

When he pulls up on the drive, Lucas grins mischievously as he notes the absence of the doctor's car. Going into the house he makes a detour to the kitchen before going up to speak with Dianna.

Helen is up to her elbows in baking, while her husband is having a mug of tea at the nearby breakfast table.

"Is everything alright?" his housekeeper asks, not expecting to see her boss until tea-time.

His grin turns conspiratorial as he explains his plan, "Alex Harvey will be turning up in the next hour to take Dianna to the hospital, but I intend to take her myself." Lucas is pleased to see the older couple smile and nod in agreement, and continues, "So I'll need someone to explain that his services are not needed...or whatever you think is best. Personally, I don't care what you say to the bloody man!"

"Not to worry...I'll make sure he understands," Helen nods, pursing her lips.

"Good, then I'll see you both later," Lucas grins.

Knocking on her bedroom door, Lucas waits to hear someone shout, "Come in" before he enters Dianna's bedroom.

"Lucas, I thought you were at work today," Dianna says, when he crosses the room towards her. "Is there something wrong?"

"Not at all..." he tells her brightly, "...I'm here to take you for your hospital appointment; time to get that cast off your leg."

"But Alex..." Dianna begins hesitantly.

"Is unable to make it," Lucas lies unashamedly. "Sorry if you're disappointed."

But to his surprise, Dianna shakes her head and smiles up at him, "I'm not disappointed in the least. It will be lovely to have you take me if you're sure you're not too busy. I could take a taxi," she offers, secretly hoping he won't take her up on it.

"No need. I'm here and I'm happy to take you. Now..." he looks over at Nurse Baxter and smiles, "...if you could get Dianna a cardigan, it's a bit on the chilly side today."

When she is fully dressed and ready, Lucas sweeps Dianna up in his arms and carries her from the bedroom.

Mmm, you smell like heaven, Lucas smiles to himself. And you feel good in my arms, though we need to feed you up a bit, you are way to light.

"I'm going to take you to lunch after we get this cast off you," Lucas announces, and waits in case Dianna wants to protest. But when she doesn't he continues, "First we'll buy you some shoes – I forgot to ask Helen to bring some when we fetched your clothes from the cottage."

Dianna is enjoying being hugged to Lucas' broad chest, and breathes in the masculine scent of him. She can feel his heart pound against her cheek. "Couldn't we stop by the cottage now; I'm sure I have some low heeled shoes that would be suitable?"

But Lucas just shakes his head, "Time enough for that when you're more prepared. It won't take much effort to nip into a shoe shop and get you a new pair."

As they reach the bottom of the stairs, Helen comes into the hallway. "Will you be having lunch with us?" she asks Lucas.

"No, I'm planning on taking Dianna out to lunch," Lucas smiles, and sees his housekeepers look of approval.

"Very well. I'll be making a lovely evening meal with a special pudding..." she smiles at Dianna, "...to celebrate you getting back on your feet."

"Thank you," Dianna smiles shyly, very aware of her position in Lucas' arms. "I'm hoping I won't be a burden to you all for much longer." Then Dianna feels Lucas' arms tighten about her and she looks up, momentarily startled.

"I don't see any need to hurry the process," he tells her sternly. "You have never been a burden, and now that you've physically recovered you may need to consider counselling."

"Counselling...?"

"Oh yes..." Helen agrees quickly, "...you won't want to go back to that house unprepared. It won't be as easy as you might think."

"Is it bad? I mean..." Visions of the cottage in terrible disarray and with her blood splattered on every surface fill Dianna's active imagination. It wouldn't be the first time she has had to clean up after one of Davey's bouts of uncontrolled anger.

Both Lucas and Helen know exactly what she means. And yes, it had been bad when they had gone to the cottage to get Dianna some clothes and her slippers. But while Helen had gathered up what she thought Dianna would need during her stay with them, Lucas had tackled cleaning up the blood that had pooled on the kitchen floor and was spattered about the living room. The cottage had looked like the scene of a very violent home invasion.

"We've taken care of it," Lucas assures her. "But if the cottage gave any indication of what you went through that day, I'd say counselling is a good idea."

"I...well...I'll have to think about that," Dianna agrees, and snuggles closer to Lucas without realising.

On the drive to the hospital, Lucas tries to distract Dianna from her contemplations. "Where would you like to go for lunch? I know a lovely riverside restaurant if you trust me to choose?"

Pulling herself out of her morose thoughts, Dianna smiles vaguely, "That sounds wonderful."

During the process of removing the plaster cast, Dianna asks that Lucas stay with her. He does so willingly, and realises that she is very nervous.

"It won't hurt..." he assures her, "...I had one myself a few years back, on my arm."

"You did?" Dianna asks, deliberately keeping her eyes on Lucas while the nurses work on her leg. And then she lets out a deep sigh. "Oooo, that feels good."

Smiling at the look of sheer bliss on her face, Lucas gets to see Dianna's leg for the first time. There is some obvious scarring where the operation was performed to repair the bone that her husband had purposely kicked and broken.

Seeing her look of distress, Lucas takes her hand, "Don't worry about the scarring. We'll get the best plastic surgeons to look at it."

But Dianna is shaking her head. "It isn't the scars...it's

the reality of it." Then tears start to fall and her heart breaks, "Oh Davey...Davey..."

Shocked and hurt by Dianna's longing for her abusive husband, Lucas can only sit by and watch as a nurse offers comfort.

How can she still be pining for him? He put those scars on her leg...he beat her to a pulp and almost cost Dianna her life! What the hell is going on!

"Thank you," Dianna sniffs and takes the box of tissues the nurse is holding out to her. "I wasn't expecting to feel this way. I don't know what's wrong with me."

Now Lucas stands and retakes her hand, "This is why I think you need to consider working through some sort of counselling."

With a breath shuddering out of her, Dianna nods in agreement, "Ok. But I can't think about it right now. I just want to get out of here."

Then Lucas realises his mistake. "Could we borrow a wheelchair to save Dianna walking back to the car in bare feet? I'm afraid my plan to buy you new shoes after getting your cast off didn't take account of getting from here to the shoe shop."

This actually brings a smile to Dianna's face. "I didn't think of it either, so we're a right pair of dunder-heads together."

A porter arrives soon after and he cheerfully wheels Dianna out to the car park, talking his inane talk and cracking a few jokes along the way.

Smiling, she thanks the porter and Lucas lifts her into the passenger side of his car. "That will be my last ride in one of those," Dianna chuckles when Lucas climbs in behind the wheel. "It's such a relief to feel normal again."

"You'll feel even more normal when we get you some shoes," Lucas observes, happy to see Dianna's smile and relaxed demeanour. "There's a small shopping centre on the outskirts of town – it'll make parking near the shop easier and less embarrassing for you."

They have to circle around a bit to get a parking spot right near the shop, but Dianna is relieved when Lucas spies someone leaving and he nips the car neatly into the vacated slot.

"Ok, my lady, your lift awaits," Lucas grins down at Dianna as she rolls her eyes at him.

But she reaches up to twine her arms about his neck as he scoops her out of the car. Turning, he uses his well toned bottom to close the car door then presses the button on his key fob to lock it.

Unable to help herself, Dianna breathes Lucas in and snuggles her head onto his shoulder, loving the warmth and feel of him.

They get a few odd looks and one or two curious smiles as they cross the short distance to enter the shoe shop. The assistants just about manage to hide their hilarity, and a young woman asks if she may help them.

Having seated Dianna on a chair, Lucas gives the young woman a smile and a nod. "We came straight from the hospital – Dianna just had a cast removed from her leg and we forgot to bring shoes for her to wear afterwards. So...here we are."

"Well, at least it was a happy event," the young woman smiles at Dianna. "What kind of shoes would you like to look at?"

But Dianna already has her eyes fixed on a pair and her face looks almost dreamy. "Aren't they gorgeous?" she asks no one in particular. "I don't think I've ever seen such beautiful shoes."

Following Dianna's gaze, both Lucas and the assistant turn to look at what has captured her attention.

"Oh," the assistant smiles and nods in agreement. "They're Carl Dersinger shoes – his designs are very popular."

Bright red, 4 inch stilettos, stand beckoning to her on a shelf. "They're so lovely, could I try them on?"

"Just tell me your size and I'll get them for you," the assistant tells her.

"5, I'm a size 5," Dianna smiles up, then notices Lucas' look of disbelief. "What?" she asks, feeling embarrassed by his scrutiny.

"I don't think I've ever seen a woman go into such raptures over a pair of shoes," he confesses with a raised brow. "Wouldn't you be better off with a pair of those," and he points to a pair of flat loafers in black.

Just then the young assistant comes back with the stilettos for Dianna to try on and they fit like a glove.

"Now try walking in them," Lucas tells her sceptically.

Lifting her chin, Dianna gets unsteadily to her feet but doesn't dare try to walk. Looking down, she can't help the sigh that escapes her. Then she sits back down, takes one last look at the beautiful shoes and slips them off.

"Ok, I have to admit, I'm not ready for heels yet," she grimaces up at the assistant. "Do you have a 5 in those?" Dianna asks, trying not to grimace.

Back in the car, Dianna has to concede that the black loafers are comfortable and easy to walk in.

"You're so practical," she states, trying her best not to sound like she's whingeing.

"Just give it a couple of weeks of regular walking to build your leg strength up and you'll be able to wear heels again," he tells her confidently.

Their lunch is a lovely relaxed affair; Dianna just loves being out with people again, the normality of it.

"You're people watching," Lucas smiles indulgently.

"I feel like I've been let out of prison," Dianna grins over at him, her eyes sparkling with glee. "I can't thank you enough for bringing me here; you've been so kind to me, Lucas."

The last comment was said sincerely enough, but Lucas is sure he heard a note of uncertainty in her voice. "Why am I hearing a 'but' on the end of that sentence?

"I don't know what you mean," Dianna lies, not yet ready to face her conflicted feelings about Lucas. For now, she just wants to enjoy the moment. "You have been kind to me. Kinder than you needed to be – which tells me you have a big heart."

Lucas can tell when a woman is being evasive, but he is also enjoying the moment and decides to let it pass. "You seem to have an admirer in Dr Harvey," he observes while sipping his tea. "Is that a mutual admiration?" he asks while watching her closely for a reaction.

"He is wonderful," Dianna enthuses, much to Lucas' annoyance, though he hides it well. "And I am full of admiration for him. He works such long hours; and you've seen how kind he is to give up some of his precious free time spending it with me. I'm sure he has a lot better things he could be doing."

You have no idea, no inkling of the man's attraction to you. Can you really be as naive as you appear...?

CHAPTER SEVEN

The garden is bright with colour and sunshine and Dianna's heart is feeling light and full of hope.

"You seem very chipper," Alex observes happily. "How about going for a drive, it's a great day for spending time outdoors?"

"I'd love to. But, Alex..." Dianna hesitates, "...you really don't have to spend your precious time off with me. I'm getting about so much better now, and you must have nicer things to do than ferry me around."

"Actually, I can't think of anything I'd like to do more," Alex assures her. "Come on, let's drive to the park and take a walk."

Taking the hand he is holding out to her, Dianna smiles happily and gets to her feet. "I'll just let Helen know that we're going out."

The housekeeper is busy in the kitchen, her hands kneading dough on a marble work surface.

"Hi..." Helen greets Dianna with a warm smile which fades quickly upon seeing Alex walk into the kitchen behind her, "...is something wrong?"

"No, not at all," Dianna replies, somewhat surprised by the kindly housekeeper's reaction to Alex's presence. "I just wanted to let you know that Alex is taking me out to the park. And I just wondered, if you might have some bread going spare for the ducks," she finishes with a shy smile.

"As it happens..." Helen's smile returns to its usual warmth, "...I was going to put these crusts out for the birds. You might as well enjoy feeding them to the ducks in the park."

Taking the bag that the housekeeper is holding out to her, Dianna thanks her. "It's such a lovely day, and I can't tell you how wonderful it feels to be walking without that heavy cast on."

"I imagine it still feels a bit strange. Will you be back for lunch?" Helen asks, a curious lift to her brows.

"Oh yes, I don't want to take up all of Alex's day off. And I have a few things I'd like to do later this morning," Dianna smiles, though it looks a little forced to the housekeeper. "I have to think and do for myself now that

Nurse Baxter has gone — she organised me so well and without me even noticing."

"Yes, she was a good sort," Helen concedes. "Alright then, you get off and enjoy the park but mind you don't try doing too much." Helen turns back to kneading the ball of dough with a little more gusto.

Sitting in Alex's car, Dianna suddenly feels even more shy than usual and keeps her head turned to look out of the passenger side window.

"You're very quiet," Alex observes after a few minutes of silence. "Aren't you feeling up to a trip out?"

"I suppose I just feel a bit guilty," Dianna admits. "I know doctors work long hours, so it doesn't feel right for you to spend what little time off you have with me."

Frowning curiously, Alex glances over at his passenger and shakes his head in bafflement. "You really don't think you're worth anyone's time," he states softly. "But you couldn't be more wrong."

When he pulls into the car park, Alex takes off his seatbelt and turns to face Dianna. "I spend time with you because I enjoy your company, Dianna. You are a very lovely person, and I find myself drawn to you."

Not used to the attentions of men, Dianna finds herself blushing with embarrassment. "Thank you."

"You're not on your own, Dianna..." Alex assures her,

"...and you don't need to feel reliant on Mr Forrester. I would be more than happy to be of assistance to you should you need it. I care for you, Dianna, and isn't that what friends are for?"

Maybe I should try and put a little distance between myself and Lucas. I can't seem to control my own body around him. I've never responded like that to any man; he's dangerous for me, of that I'm sure.

Trying to concentrate on work, Lucas buries his head in the plans for expanding the quarry. His father had always hoped to do it, but at the time planning permission had been withheld.

With the economy downturn, Lucas feels now is a good time to go up against the planning department again. After all, his business is booming and with the expansion would come more jobs for local people.

Surely even the bureaucrats on the City Council can see the sense in that! Our exports are up almost 40% on last year and our home market is 15% up. The way the orders are coming in, we should see a decent increase next year also.

"Are you going to get Mackie in to submit the plans to the planning office?" Hank asks.

"No, I'm going to do it myself!" Lucas growls firmly. "If they want to turn me down they can do it to my face. This town needs more jobs; this expansion will give a much needed boost to the local economy. With every new job comes spending power, local shop owners will feel the benefit as well as other areas of local commerce."

"You're right," Hank agrees, then sighs heavily. "We're losing our youth. Too many of them are out of work and relocating to give themselves a better chance of finding a job. I'd think the City Council would be glad of any opportunity to put a stop to the exodus."

"Yeah. George Oakley said his son is planning to leave with his girlfriend at the end of next month," Lucas informs his foreman. "Apparently his wife, Cynthia, isn't taking it too well. According to George she's been in tears over it."

"I spoke to George earlier today – he said Cynthia suggested they move to wherever the lad moves. He said she'd do anything to keep the family together," Hank frowns, shaking his head in sympathy.

"George is one of our most experienced workers..." Lucas frowns over at Hank; "...do you think he'll go along with his wife and move?"

Pursing his lips, Hank again shakes his head, "I honestly don't know. But I wouldn't blame him if he did. It isn't just the thought of losing their son that's got Cynthia all turned around – she's looking to the future when the grandchildren start arriving and she's thinking that they'll be too far away to be fully involved."

For a moment Lucas just stares back at Hank, then gets to his feet and crosses the room to look at the folder with the shift rosters in.

Flicking pages, he goes over the immediate orders in his head and tries to figure out where manpower could be effectively increased.

"George's son is around 22, 23," Lucas thinks out loud while still going through the rosters. "And I haven't heard anything bad about him – no idiotic pranks, or acting out."

"No...Carl's a good lad. He'll be 23 just before they leave next month," Hank informs him. "George said his lad is only staying around that long to please his mother. Cynthia broke down in tears when she thought he was leaving before his birthday."

"Ok..." Lucas shows the file to Hank and points out a couple of spots that could do with filling, "...get George in here and let's have a talk. I think we can help each other out and keep one of our best workers. While you fetch him in, I'll keep looking at these shift patterns and see what else I can come up with."

It takes a while to track George down and get him back to the site office. But Hank manages to do so, though George looks worried as hell.

"I told you, George, this is nothing to worry about," Hank reassures the frowning man yet again. "Lucas just wants to discuss a few possibilities to do with covering orders."

"So you say." George's gravelly voice sounds unconvinced and he straightens his spine as if going into battle as Hank opens the office door and ushers him inside.

"Take a seat, George," Lucas invites distractedly, still frowning over the work rosters and also flipping pages in the order book.

Taking a seat on the opposite side of his boss' desk, George quietly watches Lucas puzzle something out.

Minutes pass and Hank gives a discreet cough. Lucas looks up at George as though surprised.

"Sorry. Sorry. I've been trying to marry up the manpower we currently have with the orders we have and are expecting in," Lucas explains.

"So you're not letting me go?" George asks, deciding to get his fears out of the way right up front.

"What?!" Lucas looks up at Hank with a questioning frown then back at George when Hank just shakes his head. "As a matter of fact, we were discussing the possibility that you might be letting us go, as it were," Lucas lifts an enquiring brow at George.

Colouring slightly, George doesn't pretend that he doesn't understand but shifts uncomfortably in his seat. "It's not like I'd want to leave..." he begins to explain, "...but the lad is making plans to move to Nottingham. He thinks he'll stand more of a chance of finding work," George finishes sadly.

"And what do you think – do you think he should leave Ireton?" Lucas asks, interested in George's opinion of his son's plans.

"I don't like it," George shakes his head sadly. "But what can I say – the lad's been looking for work since he finished college, and apart from a few agency jobs he hasn't been able to get anything permanent."

For a long moment Lucas just looks at George and considers, then he explains his idea. "You started at this quarry under my father and I know he thought highly of you," Lucas begins, and George gives a rumbling 'hmm'.

"So the last thing I want to do is lose your skills and reliability when you move to be near your son," Lucas points out bluntly.

When George doesn't deny the possibility, Lucas decides to lay his cards on the table, "What would you think to having Carl work at the quarry? Would it cause any father and son issues?" Lucas asks insightfully.

Looking taken aback, George eventually shakes his

head and looks at his boss wide eyed and dumbfounded.

"Ok. Now we just need to know how Carl would feel about working here," Lucas looks up at Hank and nods. "I want you to interview him, if he's interested, and show him around the site. He might think differently when he realises that quarry work isn't just about driving monster trucks around all day!"

Chuckling softly, Hank nods and moves to his desk to check his diary. "We've got a lot on tomorrow and Friday – prospective buyers who want to take a look at our operation before placing sizeable orders," Hank frowns over at Lucas.

Turning to George, Lucas asks, "Can you contact Carl now? If he can get here this afternoon, around 4, we can do the interview and get this sorted!"

"You really mean you'd give my lad a job?" George asks, not quite willing to believe his own ears.

"If he's keen enough and doesn't mind helping out where he's needed, sure I'll give him a job," Lucas smiles and nods. "And if I can get the plans for the quarry expansion passed I'll be glad to take on more of the local youth. Ireton can't keep losing its younger generation to other towns, and it's time the City Council realised that!"

"Well, you know my Cynthia, always ready to fight for a cause," George chuckles, finally relaxing. "If anyone can make the Council see the error of refusing the expansion it will be my wife!"

With a broad smile Lucas stands and offers the older man his hand across the desk. When George stands and shakes it Lucas says, "Get your lad on the phone asap, then we can get things finalised."

Just as George makes to step out of the office door, Lucas calls to him. "Didn't your lad get himself engaged recently?"

"Ey' he did," Bill confirms with a curious frown.

"Is she working?"

"Nope."

"Ok, tell Carl to bring her with him — we need someone to help in the canteen if she's interested and we can do both interviews at the same time."

With a grin that couldn't get any wider, George nods and says, "I'll do that. Thanks boss."

"That was a good thing you just did," Hank smiles at Lucas. "This has always been a close community, but the recession has hit it hard."

"Then let's get our heads down on these proposals and put our argument together," Lucas tells him, a look of fierce determination in his eyes. "If the City Council want a battle, I want us to be ready to give them one they won't easily walk away from."

"Sounds like Cynthia would be a good ally from a community standpoint," Hank nods. "If we can get them behind us even before we make the application, it would add weight to the validity of the project."

With a cynical sneer, Lucas leans back in his seat, "And it just so happens to be an election year — if the community is behind us saying no could put their own jobs on the line."

"True. It would do some of those fat-cat councillors good to know what it feels like to be broke and out of work," Hank observes just as cynically.

They have both lived in Ireton all of their lives and have watched as the once thriving community has been gradually ground down.

Many youngsters in their 20's have never worked and most were looking to move away in search of jobs; just like George and Cynthia's son. But Lucas will halt the exodus if he can.

Expansion of the quarry is not just a selfish ambition to fulfil his father's dream. Lucas wants to put life back into their small town, to put wages in new pockets that would in turn put money into local businesses. He wants the youth of today to be the parents of the next generation of Ireton's children, to put new life-blood into Ireton's future.

The number of council houses with boarded up windows is growing like a plague and the spirits of those left behind are heavy with the burden of watching their community die a slow, drawn out death.

"I believe in this town, in the people who live here..." Lucas muses softly, "...so this fight could turn nasty. Our friend, Spencer, is still on the council and he's always been against anything my father wanted to do. I've always suspected there was something personal behind their animosity, but my father would never talk about it."

"Can't say I ever heard anything," Hank frowns thoughtfully.

"Me either, it was just a feeling I got when my parents talked about him...or the fact that they didn't." Lucas is now also frowning, trawling through memories and trying to recall the strange atmosphere that he'd sensed as a boy.

"I don't know..." Lucas sighs heavily, "...maybe I'm just remembering things wrong. Rob Spencer's probably just a dyed-in-the-wool bastard who abuses the power of the council that local people put him on!"

"So far that abuse hasn't cost the local people much in the way of personal loss. At the time your father was refused planning permission for expanding the quarry, local jobs weren't in such short supply. Now would be a very different prospect," Hank begins to pace the site office and consider that fact.

"What's going on in that brain of yours?" Lucas asks when his friend continues to pace silently.

"I think we should capitalise on George's idea before you submit the expansion plans," Hank muses, still pacing and thinking things through in his mind. "I think we should start lobbying the locals to get them onside. We'd be finding out what 'the people' of Ireton really want and then putting that forward to the council along with the plans."

Pursing his lips, Lucas considers the idea. "Could be a risky strategy. If the locals decide they'd rather keep the fields neighbouring the quarry for its natural beauty, we could be opening ourselves up to a protest rally rather than a support network."

Stopping in front of Lucas' desk, Hank frowns down at his friend and boss like he's just realised the man is crazy and actually voices that opinion. "Are you crazy? You've seen how devastated George was at the prospect of his son moving away, and you know of many other families that have already had their sons and daughters move away." Hank shakes his head in wonderment, "If we get the expansion passed it would mean jobs for so many people, male and female; how could anyone object to that?!"

"I'd bet my last pound that Spencer will," Lucas grins suddenly. "But I like your idea. We'll set up a meeting at George's place, if he agrees, and ask Cynthia to work her magic. She's a member of so many social circles and women's groups she'd be our ace in the hole."

"There's bound to be some green group that gets up some kind of a protest – you might even attract some outsiders; but all in all, you and your father have a terrific track record for re-establishing the wildlife and restoring old quarry works back to habitable green-space," Hank attests proudly.

"That's always been important, to both my father and me," Lucas confirms. "The land is providing us with a living; it's our duty to restore it."

CHAPTER EIGHT

Arriving home from work, Lucas walks into the kitchen to find Helen and Bill talking together with concern written clearly on their faces.

Coming to a halt, Lucas looks at the pair and his smile slips, "What's wrong – you both look like something bad has happened...so what is it?"

Glancing at each other, Bill and Helen hesitate then Bill gives Helen a go ahead nod. "It's Dianna-"

Before she can utter another word, Lucas pales and demands, "Where is she? What's happened?"

"Dianna is fine," Helen assures him hurriedly. "But she's in the process of leaving."

"What?!" Lucas stands looking from his housekeeper to her husband as if she is speaking in a foreign language that he can't understand. "What the hell are you talking about?!"

Helen takes a deep breath then fills him in on the day's events. "Dr Harvey-"

"Shit!" Lucas explodes, then apologises. "Sorry, I should have known that smarmy bastard would be involved in this somewhere!"

"Well, apparently he feels that Dianna has been reliant on you for long enough," Helen begins again. "He took Dianna out to the park this morning – I gave her some crusts to feed to the ducks and she assured me that she would be back for lunch." Helen frowns and lets out a huff of breath, "Less than an hour later, Dianna telephoned to say that she wouldn't be back after all, that Alex was taking her to lunch instead."

With hands now on her hips, her face like thunder, Helen lifts her chin and says, "I told her, thank you for letting me know and wished her a pleasant day out. But when she got back Dianna was different. Troubled and determined to leave." Then Helen shakes her head, "I tried to talk her out of it, to at least wait until you got home, and she finally agreed."

"Thank you for that," Lucas gives his housekeeper a nod and the merest smile. "Is Dianna in her room?"

"She is," Helen confirms quietly.

Walking back into the hallway, Lucas slowly mounts the oak staircase and moves to stand outside of Dianna's bedroom.

Just stay calm and play it cool. The last thing she needs is you going off on one and frightening her again.

Knocking on the door, he listens for her invitation to enter. When he does, Lucas takes a steadying breath before striding into the room.

Sat on the balcony, Dianna smiles across the room at him, though he can see how shaky her smile is.

"I hear you're planning to leave us," he tells her, and watches the shaky smile vanish.

"I can't stay here forever..." Dianna replies nervously, "...and Alex thinks it would be good for me to face up to going home sooner rather than later."

"Really," he drawls derisively. "So this is all down to the good doctor."

Feeling her cheeks flush, Dianna lifts her chin, "No, it was just a suggestion that Alex made and I happen to agree with. He thinks the longer I put off going home the harder it will be to do so."

Then Lucas surprises her by agreeing. "True, very true; but to rush into doing so without any preparation would be foolhardy in the extreme."

Feeling her cheeks heat with temper this time, Dianna gets to her feet, "I am not a fool. I know how hard it will be to walk back into that house, to realise that Davey will never come home to me again. But that doesn't mean I'm not strong enough to face it."

Looking over to the bed, Lucas can see that she has already packed a suitcase that he can only assume Helen has lent her. "I see you've already made up your mind." Stiffening, he crosses to the bed and picks up the suitcase then looks back at Dianna, "I'll take you home, since you obviously can't stand to be here another minute longer than you have to be."

Moving forward, Dianna reaches out to touch his arm, then withdraws her hand as if she has been burned. "Please don't be angry. You've been so kind, and I've loved staying here. I want to thank you for all the time and care that you've given me, for all the expense that you've been put to in hiring Nurse Baxter and for my keep," she tells him quietly. "Can't we at least part as friends?"

When his slate grey eyes look down into hers, Dianna feels her heart contract with sadness. "Friends...yes, we can part as friends, because that's all you have the courage to accept," he tells her bitterly. "But if you think running away, putting distance between us, will quell what we feel then you really are a fool."

Watching him stride out of the room, Dianna slowly follows and sadly closes the door behind her.

He doesn't just drop her off on the street as Dianna requested, but carries her suitcase round the back of the cottage and lets Dianna scuttle after him with arms full of things that hadn't fit into the case.

Putting the suitcase down at the back door, he turns to Dianna and watches as her knees give way.

"God damn it!" Crossing the small gap between them in record time, Lucas catches her to him before Dianna can hit the ground along with her belongings. "I knew this was a bad idea. Now will you come back with me?!"

He can feel her body shake as she leans into him for support, but after a moment Dianna straightens and pulls out of his arms.

"I'll be fine. Alex is right, I have to face up to this to be able to move on with my life."

Biting back a nasty comment, Lucas picks up the fallen objects and walks at Dianna's side watching for any sign that she might faint.

With hands trembling, she fits a key into the lock, they are positively shaking when Dianna turns the handle and opens the back door.

In a flash of time she is back there, hearing Davey's shouts and feeling his fists pummelling her face and body.

A hand moves instinctively to cover her stomach, the slight swell reassuring as she remembers all too well her desperate pleas that he not hurt their baby.

Miracle of miracles, she had woken in the hospital to

the news that the baby had survived; she was still pregnant.

As she steps into the kitchen Dianna's eyes sweep the room expecting to find blood and disorder, overturned chairs and broken pots, but there is nothing to give a clue to the horrors that had taken place just a few short weeks ago.

"Did you do this? Did you bring Helen here to clean my house?" Dianna asks, her voice sounding strange even to her own ears.

"We had to come to get you some clothes and a few necessities, as Helen put it," Lucas informs her.

"Thank her for me, will you?" Dianna asks, and goes through to the sitting room with a little less dread in her heart.

He'd allowed Dianna to think that Helen had been the one to clean her blood from the kitchen floor and the splatters of it from the walls and other surfaces, but it had been Lucas who had carried out the dreadful task.

And, looking at the floor now, he can remember the gut wrenching anger that had gripped him when he thought of how it had come to be there.

I didn't even know you then, but to find out what had been done to you was enough to make any man seethe. It was a good job that Davey was already dead; I'd have swung for him that day I found you here. Broken...barely clinging to life...

"I'm sorry..." Dianna begins softly, watching his pale face relive his own horrific memories of that day, "...I didn't think...I should have known this would be difficult for you too."

Shaking his head, dismissing the memories, Lucas turns to Dianna and is surprised to see her dry eyed.

"You're stronger than I gave you credit for," he tells her, pulling his lips into a good facsimile of a smile. "Perhaps I have been holding you back."

"If you have, I know it was well intentioned." And Dianna walks to him, takes his hand and brings it to her lips. "You've been so thoughtful and so kind to someone you didn't even know. But I will manage; I will get back on my feet and build a life without Davey."

Seeing the sadness cast shadows in her eyes, Lucas gently pulls her to him and simply holds her there. "You don't need to do this all by yourself; I'm only a phone call away."

"I will call; just give me time to find my feet and I will call," she tells him softly.

Leaving her there alone is one of the hardest things Lucas has ever had to do. It goes against all his better instincts, but Dianna has made her choice clear.

The following week passes in a blur; Lucas buries himself in the plans he's drawn up for the quarry. The interview with Carl and his fiancée, Joanna, had gone well and both are now employed full time.

Cynthia has been as good as her word; the meeting at their house had turned into what amounted to a council of war and now she is putting their plans into action.

She has been spreading the word about how Lucas has helped to keep her family together and how he wants to help others in the same way.

"If he can get the expansion plans passed by the committee there will be more work for our children and they won't need to leave Ireton to make a living," Cynthia tells yet another group of women at their sewing group.

"What can any of us do?" one woman asks when Cynthia suggests they all take action in support of Lucas' plans. "They won't listen to a bunch of old women, men never do let alone men in suits!"

"Then we'll make them listen!" Cynthia outlines the plan to hold a demonstration outside the Council Offices, "But we need to wait until the quarry plans have been submitted before we do anything. Just spread the word and get as many people on side as you can."

The Town Hall is a buzz of people, far more than has ever been seen when a planning hearing is being held.

Calls for calm and quiet go ignored until Lucas stands to say his piece. With a prepared speech in his hands, Lucas begins to outline what his aims and ambitions are for the Ireton Quarry. But then he lays the paper down and turns to look at the local people all gathered to support him.

His eyes take in the faces of people who have retired from the quarry now, people who used to work alongside his father. And next to them he sees their sons and daughters, or empty seats where the sons and daughters should have been sitting, only they have left Ireton in search of work.

With his resolve strengthened, Lucas turns back to the committee and begins again. "All that I've outlined has been true enough, but this hearing will decide more than just the future of my business." Looking along the row of committee members, his slate grey eyes rest on Robert Spencer for a moment longer.

Lucas can already see the man's decision in his eyes, his face set in stone against him. "I'm asking that you think about the families here tonight; that you think about the loss of our young people because of the lack of work. Ireton needs this boost not only for its economy, but for its very existence."

"A bit dramatic, don't you think?" Robert Spencer

sneers contemptuously. "Are you seriously telling us that your plans are entirely altruistic, that profit is not your priority but the people of Ireton are?"

Steeling himself, clamping down on the temper that wants to take the lead, Lucas manages to look at Councilman Spencer with no more than reason in his eyes. "What I'm trying to tell you is that the two go hand in hand. Of course I need to make a profit; what business doesn't if it is to survive, and a healthy one at that. But the expansion will give something back to the town's people; it will give them back the promise of a future with their families at the heart of it."

"A boy died at your quarry..." Spencer sneers slyly, "...he doesn't have a future anymore."

Caught off guard, Lucas has to take a moment to pull his thoughts together. "That was an unforeseeable tragedy, and one I won't go into in public."

"And why not..." Spencer persists unpleasantly, "...are you afraid the people and the committee will learn about your safety measures — or lack of them?" he adds derisively.

Spencer's derision makes Lucas look at him — really look at him and wonder what had happened to make this man hate him so much. It had started with his father, Lucas is sure, but now it is aimed right at him. Why? What did we ever do to earn your hatred?

"The circumstances of that young man's death have been investigated thoroughly, as I'm sure you are aware," Lucas replies coolly. "And my reluctance to discuss it here is out of respect for his family."

"The boy died while working for you – are you telling us that that has got nothing to do with you? That you and your 'profits'..." Spencer almost spits the word, "...bare no responsibility for his loss of life!"

The anger in Lucas' belly is mixed with regret, and yes a good helping of guilt. The boy had been working for him, he'd know that Davey had problems and had thought he'd helped the boy to turn his life around. But maybe I was wearing blinkers where Davey was concerned – I certainly never pegged him as a wife beater. So what else did I get wrong...?

"That's enough!" a woman demands from the back of the hall. Every head turns to watch as she walks to the front of the crowd to face the committee. "I've known many of you all of my life..." she tells the committee, looking from one to the other along the table they are seated at, "...and I'm here to tell you that this man saved my life."

A collective gasp goes up and the nearest Councillor to her asks, "Dianna, how is this relevant to the current hearing? We are discussing the plans submitted by Mr Forrester for the expansion of his quarry works."

"It is relevant because you were just discussing the death of my husband, Davey Linden," Dianna turns her eyes to glare at Robert Spencer. Then turning to face Lucas, she smiles tentatively, "I believe you were trying to save my embarrassment by not telling these people what Davey did to me and why he died that day. But I can't let you take the blame for something that was never your fault," Dianna sighs, her hands clasped tightly together in front of her.

Looking around the room, she sees curious stares looking back at her, but also sympathetic eyes that have guessed her secret.

"I think some of you might have suspected that something was wrong in my marriage to Davey," she begins quietly. "The odd bruise that you asked after, worried that I'd hurt myself," Dianna smiles at a woman in the third row, remembering her kind concern. "But then they appeared more frequently and became difficult to explain away." Stopping to pull in a breath, Dianna turns her eyes to Lucas.

"You don't have to do this," he tells her, his heart filled with admiration for her courage and sense of honour.

But Dianna strengthens her resolve and turns back to the row of Councilmen and continues with her story. "Davey had been struggling with his daily life and the responsibilities that being married entailed. It wasn't that he was a cruel man, but he was a weak man and took that weakness out on me."

It hurts her to admit as much to herself, let alone voice her opinion to a crowd of people. But these are not strangers – Ireton is a small town and she knows most of the faces looking back at her in one way or another and also knows that they care about her.

"Davey had become a drug user..." another collective gasp goes up and a small amount of chatter ensues then quiets, "...I think he used them as a crutch when things got on top of him. But when Lucas found out about it he didn't just sack Davey, he paid his wages for six months while his foreman, Hank Fisher, went with Davey to support meetings and helped him to get clean. And he was clean..." Dianna lifts her chin with pride, "...he worked hard to be the man he truly wanted to be, but life became too hard when he found out he was to be a daddy."

The women in the crowd gasp and sigh, some of them nodding with understanding.

With a hand on her stomach, Dianna continues, "By

some miracle, and due in no small part to the help and support of Lucas Forrester, not only did I survive being beaten to within an inch of my life but my baby survived the attack too."

A happy cheer goes up and many women's faces become wet with tears.

"Davey was found to have taken a lot of drugs that day. I had no idea he still had any, or maybe he got hold of some after leaving me for dead on our kitchen floor," Dianna tells them, her bottom lip beginning to tremble and puts a finger to it to steady her.

"I loved Davey, and I don't want any of you to think badly of him just because he couldn't cope with the everyday stresses of life. Not all men are made strong, and not all women make good wives."

Hearing Lucas' loud oath makes Dianna turn to him again. "There are always two sides to every story; I'm not saying that what Davey did was right...but I don't believe he was entirely to blame either."

Shaking his head in exasperation, Lucas remains quiet for Dianna's sake. He doesn't want to hurt her; she's putting herself through this ordeal for him.

"I do believe in Lucas Forrester," Dianna states firmly, looking at the crowd of locals and then to each of the Councillors in turn. "And I believe in Ireton, that we can save our community if we give the quarry a chance to grow and provide work for our youth!"

Turning her eyes back to the crowd she watches as they get to their feet and cheer, with calls of 'give the lad a chance' and 'save our town' ringing in her ears.

When she looks back at Lucas, he seems taken aback by it all, but then smiles and nods his thanks to the people gathered to support him.

CHAPTER NINE

Opening her eyes, Dianna sees that the sun is shining on a new day. It is only 6 a.m. but she is wide awake and not entirely sure that she is ready for the day ahead.

Alex is due to call round at lunch time, but Dianna isn't sure how she feels about that.

At first he had been kind and understanding; now he is becoming more demanding, expecting her to face her past and move on from it.

But it isn't that easy. I always loved this cottage — when Davey and I bought this place I saw us getting old here...together. It just doesn't mean the same anymore, and holds so many bad memories that the good ones are hard to recall.

Lucas was right, it has been hard coming back here. I wish I had somewhere else I could be, and I wish I'd listened to Lucas about the counselling – I didn't think I'd feel so haunted by my past, but it dogs my every waking hour.

Climbing into the shower, Dianna allows herself to enjoy the heat and relaxes as much as she is able. Massaging shower gel into her skin feels good and she takes her time in doing so.

But then her thoughts turn to the night before, to Lucas and his meeting with the planning committee.

He was so stupid. He might have lost the approval he needed just to save my pride. As for Robert Spencer, well...he didn't get the verdict he'd obviously been angling for; the slimy bastard!

How could he try using Davey's death to score off Lucas?! The man is less than human...less than a slug!

I'm glad I decided to go along. Ok I didn't think I'd be standing up there giving a speech, but I'm very glad that I did.

The look on Lucas' face had been worth any embarrassment she might have suffered. But in fact, many of the town's people had congratulated her and offered to help out in any way she might need.

That's what's so precious about Ireton...the people and the sense of community. I'm not alone, and neither is anyone else in need.

Later that morning, after cleaning through the house yet again, as if trying to clean out all the bad memories, Dianna takes her coffee to the breakfast table and pulls out a chair to sit on.

"Oh! Oh my God!"

Horrified, Dianna stands transfixed by a single drop of dried blood that had obviously been missed by Helen. Only when the hot drink spills onto her hand does Dianna realise that she is shaking badly and quickly crosses to the sink to put her mug into it.

A knock at the door has her jumping in alarm and her eyes swiftly turn to the clock.

It can't be Alex, it's too soon.

As her thoughts whirl around in her head Dianna hears another, more urgent knock on the front door.

On automatic pilot, Dianna crosses to open it and finds Lucas standing there.

His smile slips on seeing her, and instead of handing her the bouquet of flowers that he'd brought to thank her, Lucas pushes inside and discards the flowers on the nearby settee.

"What's happened? What's wrong?" Lucas demands, his hands on her shoulders and his eyes looking over her for signs of injury.

Dianna can't get the words out, and the tears she still

hasn't realised she is shedding just keep rolling down her pale cheeks. But she does manage to raise an arm and points to the kitchen chair.

Frowning, Lucas goes in that direction searching for anything that might have caused Dianna's distress, but he can't find anything.

"I don't understand...there's nothing here..."

"It's mine...it has to be...right there on the chair," and Dianna steps forward to point a shaky finger at the dried blood.

"Bloody hell! I thought I'd got it all," Lucas tells her unthinkingly. "Damn it, you go and sit in the lounge while I get rid of this and check for any more."

Without saying a word, Dianna obeys and waits for Lucas to finish cleaning.

She could watch him do it; the through lounge is one long room with the lounge at one end and the dining room and kitchen at the other. But Dianna sits back in her chair, using the partial wall that houses the stairs to block her view.

"You let me think it was Helen who had cleaned the house," Dianna tells him when he joins her moments later.

"It wasn't a job I'd let any woman do," Lucas dismisses easily. Then his eyes alight on her hands and a frown creases his brow. "What happened; why is your hand so red?"

Automatically, Dianna covers the sore hand with her good one and winces at the pain. "It's nothing...I just spilled my coffee a little."

But Lucas steps forward and holds out his hand for hers so as to inspect the damage. When he sees how angry the scolded skin looks he pulls her to her feet, guides her back into the kitchen and runs the cold water tap.

"Keep it under there for at least ten minutes," he instructs firmly when she would have pulled her hand away. "It'll help minimise the damage and the pain, but I want to take you to the doctor afterwards."

"No, that's ok. I'm going to the hospital soon anyway," Dianna protests. "I'll just ask one of the nurses for some advice."

"Hospital? Why are you going to the hospital?" Lucas asks full of concern again.

"The baby," Dianna smiles shyly. "It's my first visit."

Looking down at her stomach, Lucas' mouth forms a silent 'O'.

"How are you getting there – are you taking the car?" he asks, having seen the familiar red Ford Fiesta sat in front of the house.

Lowering her eyes, Dianna heaves a sigh, "Someone kindly returned Davey's car and posted the keys through the letterbox, but I don't drive. I never learned how," she tells him sadly.

It had been one more way of controlling her. When she had mentioned to Davey that she would like to take driving lessons he had scoffed and told her that it would be too much for her and that he could always take her anywhere they needed to go.

"What time is your appointment?" Lucas asks kindly, hating the sadness that has settled on her lovely face.

"10:30; I was going to call a taxi...but everything went wrong..." she tails off, feeling hopeless.

"You should have called me," he frowns down at her, but smiles to take the edge off. "I'd love to go with you, and it gives me a legitimate reason to bunk off."

With a genuine smile, Dianna angles her head up to him and says, "You...Lucas Forrester, workaholic to the core bunk off? I don't think so!"

Giving in to a deep chuckle, Lucas reaches over to turn the tap off and takes another look at her hand. "I never had a reason to bunk off before; but I can't think of a better reason than coming with you to your baby appointment."

"They're called anti-natal appointments," she informs

him. Then her smile fades and her blue eyes darken.

"Will you stop with the worrying," he tells her, reading the tell-tale signs. "If I don't care that they might think I'm the father, then you shouldn't care either."

He knows he's guessed correctly when her pale cheeks pink up prettily.

"I just don't relish the idea of explaining-"

"Then don't," he cuts her off firmly. "And besides, if they think I'm the dad they'll let me come in with you."

Shaking her head, Dianna lifts her eyes to look curiously at him, "You actually want to hear all the baby talk. I'd think it would bore you?!"

It would have bored Davey, she knew. In fact, she wouldn't have asked him to come with her to the hospital; it was something he would have expected Dianna to take care of herself.

"Bored? Not on your life! I'm sure I'll find it fascinating; after all, I want to be a dad myself one day. If I can find someone to have me, that is," and his smile is so genuine that Dianna can't bring herself to question the sincerity of it.

Only when they are sat in the waiting area of the anti-natal clinic does Dianna begin to have doubts again. She's seen the covert admiring glances that Lucas is attracting; some of them quite blatant...even from the nursing staff.

Probably wondering what such a gorgeous man is doing with a woman like me. If they only knew!

Lucas isn't fazed by any of it. He is indeed fascinated by the different sizes and shapes of the women who are waiting alongside them. It doesn't occur to him that their glances are anything more than shared curiosity; it is, he thinks, like an exclusive club where only those who are pregnant can join.

Watching a couple emerge from one of the rooms, Lucas smiles at their obvious joy. Both of them are engrossed in the photograph they are looking at, and he wonders if they've been told if it's a girl or a boy.

"Would you want to know?" he asks Dianna suddenly.

"What?" she asks confused.

"The sex of the baby; would you want to know if it's a boy or a girl?" he grins widely.

Seeing his enthusiasm chases away all of Dianna's doubts. "I'm not sure, I haven't really thought about it."

"But you could; if you get one of those photos that some of the parents have you might be able to see for yourself," he suggests happily.

"Sorry, this is only my first visit and it's too early for that kind of a scan," Dianna smiles, a little sad to see his eagerness falter.

"Oh...so no photo?"

"Not one that might show the baby's sex I'm afraid; not this time, anyway."

"Mrs Linden...?" A nurse calls out and glances over the small crowd of women for a response.

Dianna gets to her feet and smiles in acknowledgement.

Come this way, please. Dr Martin will see you today," she smiles reassuringly.

The consultation had gone well. Lucas asked lots of questions and had taken a keen interest in everything the doctor said.

"We need to get you stocked up with fresh fruit and veg'," he tells Dianna as they cross the car park to his car. "Are you taking the folic acid that he recommended? We can get you some large bananas also; they're a good source of natural folic acid, and sunflower seeds, too."

"Good Lord, you really were listening in there," Dianna chuckles kindly. "And I've been taking folic acid even when I was in the hospital, apparently."

Frowning, Lucas hesitates as he's about to unlock the car door, "How did that happen...you were unconscious for the first little while?!"

"Remember that awful tube thing I had down my nose?" she asks with a grimace. And when he nods she says, "Well they can give medicine and crushed tablets down it straight into the gut."

Lucas also grimaces, "They actually told you that?"

"I still had it in for a few days after I came round..." she reminds him, "...so I was awake while they did it."

His grimace deepens, "You were?"

"I didn't feel a thing," she chuckles again. "The worst part is the tube itself; you can feel it at the back of your throat every time you swallow. It made me gag a few times."

"Eew," he grimaces again, then unlocks the car and they both get in.

"I would never have guessed you are so squeamish," Dianna smiles over at, a slightly green around the gills, Lucas.

"I can deal, in an emergency," Lucas clarifies. "But it isn't something I'd want to cope with on an everyday basis. Christ knows how doctors do it!"

Her smile falters and a sad shadow replaces the teasing light in her eyes. "That reminds me, I need to get back and get ready. Alex is coming round this afternoon."

Having turned the ignition on, Lucas turns in his seat to face her, "Why has that thought put a frown on your face? Aren't you looking forward to Dr Do-it-all calling on you?"

Pulling back the smile she'd allowed to slip, Dianna does her best to gloss over her silly reluctance. "Alex has been great. I just worry that he's putting himself out needlessly. He has a very busy life, and adding me to it can't be easy."

With a huff, Lucas turns back to face the way ahead and pulls out of the car park.

Both of them are lost in thought and the car pulls up outside of her cottage all too soon.

"Thank you for coming with me, Lucas," Dianna smiles shyly. "It helped more than I would have thought."

"Glad to be of service," and Lucas' smile is back in place again. "Does that mean I get to come with you next time?"

Giving a light laugh, Dianna's blue eyes twinkle with happiness. "Do you really want to? Those ladies were all but eating you alive in there."

"Really?" his smile widens considerably.

"Oh you're incorrigible!" Dianna shakes her head on a laugh as she climbs out of the car. "But yes, if you would like to come with me I'd be glad of your company."

"Then I'll be there. Just let me know when," and Lucas lifts a hand in a wave then drives off.

Standing on the pavement, Dianna watches until his car disappears around a corner then turns to enter her cottage.

Why am I so anxious about Alex coming round? It's

just a visit, and he's been so kind. But he seems to expect so much, he doesn't seem to understand why I'm finding it difficult being back in the cottage again.

And I know I'm being silly getting uptight when he gets annoyed with me. Like he said, he's just trying to get me to move on, to stop looking back.

But it makes me nervous when he gets really annoyed, when I can see the irritation in his eyes and hear it in his voice. It reminds me of Davey...but that's silly. Alex would never do what Davey did, he's just looking out for me.

Never-the-less, when Dianna gets indoors she goes straight upstairs to change. Alex had commented on the blouse she is wearing, had told her that the neckline was too low for a woman of good standing to wear, so she would change it before he arrived.

There's no point wearing it if it will annoy him. And he really likes this blue one.

Pulling on the blue blouse, Dianna buttons it all the way up to the high collar. When she looks in the mirror, Dianna is happy enough with her appearance until she notices that her skirt is perhaps a little tight.

No point asking for trouble. Alex pointed out that woman in the park the other day.

'Good Lord, what is she dressed like. Low neckline, a skirt tight enough to show the line of her underwear – no wonder men get the wrong idea. Or maybe it's the right idea in her case'.

Remembering that comment, Dianna slips her pencil skirt off and pulls a roomier, gathered skirt on. "There, not a knicker line in sight," she smiles.

In the kitchen, Dianna unwraps the flowers that Lucas had brought her that morning, and finds a suitable vase to arrange them in.

Thank goodness he thought to put water in the sink; the poor things would have been withering by now if it had been left to me. I can be such a scatter-brain sometimes. And Lucas was so understanding when I went to pieces; the sight of my own blood reminded me all too vividly what had happened in this house. What had happened to me...

Alex's brisk knock on the front door had Dianna jumping ten feet off the ground, her heart racing madly, and she almost knocked the vase over.

Laughing at herself, Dianna walks to the door and pulls it open, "Hi, come on in."

"Well you look happy," Alex smiles brightly and closes the door behind him.

"It made me jump. The knock on the front door..." she explains when Alex frowns, "...I was lost in my own little world, arranging these beautiful flowers, when the knock on the door almost stopped my heart."

"They are lovely," Alex comments as he steps forward to finger a bright yellow rose petal. "What made you buy them?"

"Oh I didn't. They were a thank you gift from Lucas; though he shouldn't have gone to this expense," but Dianna's smile betrays the fact that she is pleased that he did.

"Forrester bought these...why?"

His tone wasn't angry, but Dianna can tell that he isn't best pleased.

"He had a silly idea that I'd helped him to get the planning permission he needed for expanding the quarry. But I doubt I made any difference," she dismisses modestly.

"You need to be careful there..." Alex smiles, though it doesn't reach his eyes, "...you don't want to be mistaken for one of those women who lead a man on. Forrester might think you're interested in him."

Taken aback, Dianna gapes up at him, "But that's silly, Lucas would never think like that."

"Hmm..." Alex purses his lips and again touches his fingers to the flowers, "...I'm not so sure. You were quite flirty with him when you were staying at his house. I couldn't blame the man for thinking you were throwing yourself at him."

Unable to stop her bottom lip from trembling, Dianna is mortified to think that she might have given Lucas any such idea.

Suddenly Alex's arms close around her and pull Dianna into a comforting embrace. "There, there, not to worry. I was probably the only one who noticed. Now, how about I take you out to lunch to cheer you up? You look delightful, by the way."

CHAPTER TEN

Alone in her bedroom, Dianna feels sad despite having had a lovely time with Alex. He'd taken her to a lovely restaurant where they had eaten lunch outdoors.

There had been a play area a few yards away from them and she'd been able to watch the children playing, imagining how it would feel to watch her own child at play.

She wants to feel happy, knows she should be grateful that she has such good friends to look out for her, but Dianna can't stem the tears that are soaking into her pillow.

I know you never meant to hurt me, Davey. And I know you loved me when you could. The world was just too much for you to deal with.

Her dreams were chaotic; Davey was angry, shouting

at her, frightening her. Then it was Alex, his frown telling her that he was impatient with her dwelling on the past, his words making her feel small when he told her to pull herself together and move on.

And then it was Lucas; his smile warmed her heart, made her feel good and his arms made her feel safe. But they made her feel other things too; things that she had no right to feel.

"Lucas!" Dianna woke with his name screaming from her lips, a hand grasping at her stomach. "Oh God! What is it? What's wrong?"

Curled in a fetal position, her arms wrapped tightly across her painfully cramping stomach, Dianna wakes into a living nightmare.

"No, not the baby, please God don't let it be the baby!" But the pain worsens and she can feel something warm oozing from between her legs.

It doesn't occur to her to ring Alex, even though he is a doctor. When she picks up the bedside phone it is Lucas' number she punches in.

Hearing his sleepy voice ask, "Who is it," Dianna swallows down on the pain and gasps, "Something's wrong...so much pain..."

Wide awake now, Lucas sits bolt upright in bed, "Dianna, is that you?!" But all he can hear is her desperate cry as the phone clatters to the floor.

Pulling on jeans and a jumper, Lucas runs along the landing to Helen and Bill's room and gives it a rousing knock.

In a moment, Bill comes to the door to find out what's going on and sees by the look on his employer's face that some kind of emergency is occurring.

"What is it?" he asks, all attention.

"I need Helen to come with me to Dianna's cottage – I think she's losing the baby," he sighs heavily, shakily. "She sounded like she was in a lot of pain, and that's the only thing I can think of."

Having heard the conversation Helen had pulled on some clothes and was at the door ready to leave. "You call an ambulance..." she tells her husband as she pushes past him, "...we'll get over to Dianna and stay with her till it arrives."

On the way to the cottage, Lucas speaks his thoughts out loud. "What if I'm wrong? What if it's something else? I don't know anything about babies."

"You said she was in a lot of pain," Helen reminds him. "Whatever it is, Dianna needs to go to the hospital to be checked out. There is no reason for that amount of pain during a normal pregnancy."

Once they reach the cottage, Helen and Lucas realise that they can't get in. "There's no way Dianna can make it to the door to let us in, not with the amount of pain she was in," Lucas states confidently. "Let's take a look round the back; maybe there's a window I can prise open – or failing that I'll have to smash one!"

In the end he does have to smash one, but on hearing the screams coming from the cottage he reasons he doesn't have time for pussy-footing about.

The frantic pair rush up the stairs in the direction of Dianna's terrified cries, and find her lying on a bed covered in blood, her nightdress soaked in it.

"It'll be alright," Helen sooths, smoothing the damp hair back from Dianna's sweaty brow. "An ambulance is on the way, my lovely, and we'll stay with you all the time."

"The baby..." Dianna gasps, her blue eyes looking into Helen's with a desperate plea.

"I'm sorry, Dianna, the baby is gone," Helen tells her sadly, and has to watch Dianna's heart break as understanding dawns.

At the hospital, Lucas and Helen wait in a room lined with chairs, for news of Dianna's condition.

Neither of them is making use of the seating provided; Helen is staring dejectedly out of the window while Lucas wears a groove in the floor with his pacing.

When the waiting room door finally opens, both heads

snap round to watch a doctor they had spoken to earlier enter the room.

"How is she? Did she lose the baby?" Lucas asks, not able to let go of the tiny hope he's been clinging to for Dianna's sake.

With a sad nod of his head the doctor confirms that she had. "I'm so sorry. The miscarriage had already happened before she got to us, but we took her to theatre to make sure that everything was clear and Mrs Linden is more comfortable now."

For a moment, Lucas can think about nothing but the pain Dianna had suffered and the amount of blood that she'd been covered in. But then another thought strikes him and his heart contracts painfully in his chest, "Will Dianna still be able to have children?"

"In time her body will recover and hopefully that will be a possibility," the doctor smiles uneasily. "But I note from her records that Mrs Linden has had previous trauma to her uterus that required surgery to repair; there is a chance that Mrs Linden may not be able to carry a baby to full term."

"As if she hasn't suffered enough," Helen cries, her hand flying up to cover her mouth and stifle her sobs.

Guiding his housekeeper to a chair, Lucas crosses back to the doctor and asks, "Can I see her? I need to see Dianna."

"I'll take you through to the ward, but it will be up to the Sister whether or not she allows you to see Mrs Linden," he warns Lucas.

Even dead, Davey's actions are still hurting Dianna! That bloody man may have cost her everything – even the ability to become a mother! And she was so happy when she found out her pregnancy had survived Davey's attack on her; how will Dianna ever cope with this new tragedy.

"I'll just have a quick word with the Ward Sister, if you could take a seat here," the doctor indicates a chair and then disappears from view.

"I hate hospitals," Lucas groans as he looks about the small reception area at the various posters on the yellow walls.

"Are you Lucas?" a severe looking woman in her 40's asks him.

At his nod she waves him forward, "Dianna has been asking for you, but I will ask you to stay for no longer than 10 minutes, we have a lot of other patients to think about also."

A nurse guides him over to a bed with the curtains drawn round it and parts them just enough for him to enter.

Jesus, you look so tiny in that bed. So tiny and so pale, I just want to gather you up and take you home.

"Lucas?" Her voice is a whisper, but he can hear the tears in it.

"I'm here," he tells her, and crosses to the chair at the side of her bed and takes her hand. "I'm right here."

"I've lost the baby," she tells him, her bottom lip trembling badly.

"I know, sweetheart. But at least you're ok," he soothes, and strokes her hair knowing that her heart is breaking.

"They said...they said..." tears begin to trail down Dianna's cheeks again as she tries to voice the terrible news, "...I may never be able to have children."

Then the damn breaks and her sobs rack her body as Lucas draws her to him.

"It's alright," he croons over and over, his large gentle hand smoothing over her back as he rocks her in his arms.

She all but climbs on to his knee, so he sits himself on her bed and pulls her more fully into his arms. "I'm right here, Dianna. I'm right here."

Although the nurses put a head in the curtains now and then to check that everything is alright, they don't ask Lucas to leave until Dianna is settled fast asleep and back in her bed.

Moving quietly up the dimly lit ward, Lucas stops by the nurse's station to speak to the night Sister. "What time will I be allowed to visit tomorrow?" he asks, his voice soft so as not to disturb the nearby sleeping patients.

"This card has our visiting times and contact numbers on it," the Sister replies kindly, handing him the card. "We'll keep a close eye on Mrs Linden," she assures him.

Then Lucas gives the Sister one of his business cards and tells her, "I want you to call at any hour of the day or night if Dianna needs me. And thank you, for everything you're doing for her."

Then Lucas leaves the ward and returns to Helen in the waiting room, his feet like lead as he has to once again leave Dianna in the hospital.

"I'm sorry it took so long..." he apologises when Helen gets up from her seat, "...but I just couldn't leave her when she was so upset. And she...she..."

Rubbing a hand across his tired eyes, Lucas has to stop his explanations and pull himself together.

"There now..." Helen rubs a hand up and down his arm, "...let's get home and I'll make you a nice cup of tea. Then you can tell me all about it."

The drive home doesn't take long, but when they arrive Lucas declines the offer of tea and goes up to what was Dianna's bedroom.

Closing the door behind him, Lucas walks to the

balcony and steps outside. The night air is chilly, but he doesn't feel it.

How many times had he sat here with Dianna, enjoying her laughter or soothing her tears.

Now all he can think of is her tiny body pressed into his, shuddering with the tears he'd thought would never end.

You bastard, Davey Linden! Were you alive today I'd make you pay for what you did! For all the heartache and pain you've inflicted on Dianna. I'd rip you limb from bloody limb and enjoy every moment!

For another little while, Lucas looks out over the garden awash with shadows and slivers of moonlight. Then he turns back into the room and, getting undressed, climbs into Dianna's bed.

It is small comfort to sleep where Dianna had once slept, but Lucas needs to feel close to her in any way he can.

His dreams, however, bring him no comfort at all. He is taken back to the day he first found Dianna, the day he'd looked down on her broken body with blood pooled all around her on the kitchen floor where she lay.

Tossing and turning, Lucas doesn't realise that he is calling out her name. "Dianna. Dianna, I'm here..." And when he wakes in the morning, he doesn't feel refreshed.

His head is throbbing and his body is tangled in the bedding, evidence of his restless night.

"Sod the visiting times..." he exclaims as he extricates himself from the snarled up bedding, "...I need to see Dianna right now!"

Taking a quick shower in his own room, Lucas pulls on clothes that he barely considers and forgoes breakfast in his bid to reach Dianna's side.

I suppose there'll be some dragon at the door trying to keep me out, but surely, even dragons have hearts.

I should have got Dianna a private room. Damn it, Forrester, don't you ever think! Thumping the steering wheel, he continues his journey getting more and more angry with himself.

By the time he reaches Dianna's ward, Lucas is in no mood to take any crap from anyone.

Pressing the buzzer at the outer door, Lucas waits for someone to answer.

"May I help you?" a disembodied voice asks politely.

"I need to see Dianna Linden. I know it's not visiting time, but I need to see her," he persists.

"Just one moment and Sister will be out to see you," the voice tells him, and the intercom snaps off.

Sure enough, the same Sister that had spoken to him earlier is walking towards him and opens the door to the ward.

"Come in, Mr Forrester..." she invites cordially, "...I wondered how long it would take for you to come back." Her smile is inviting, understanding and placating all at once.

"I'm sorry to intrude, but I just need to see that Dianna's ok. She doesn't have anyone else," Lucas states simply.

Putting a finger to her lips, the Sister escorts Lucas to Dianna's bed where he finds her still fast asleep.

"Jesus, how much more can one woman take?" Lucas doesn't realise he has spoken the words out loud until he sees Dianna's eyes open.

"Lucas...?" she blinks sleep away, sure that she must be dreaming.

"I'm here," Lucas moves forward quickly and sits on the side of her bed to take her hand.

The Ward Sister turns a blind eye and moves back to the nurse's station to give them some privacy.

The ward is still dimly lit, though daylight is starting to break through the windows.

"Oh Lucas..." Dianna sits up and winds her arms about his neck, "...I'm so glad you're here."

Holding her to him, Lucas is thankful that he took the risk of coming so early in the morning. "I thought I'd have to battle a dragon to get back in here so early," he grins.

"But the Sister on here is a decent sort; she had a feeling I'd be back."

"I'm so glad," Dianna repeats into his shoulder. "I wish I could go home. I hate being here. It reminds me of..." But she can't finish the dreadful thought.

"What do you say to coming home with me?" Lucas invites, still holding her to him and praying that she'll say yes. "I can get Nurse Baxter to come back for a few days and you can rest up without any worry."

Surprising him, Dianna nods eagerly. "Yes please," she whispers, then inexplicably bursts into tears.

"Hey, hey, that wasn't meant to upset you," Lucas grins down into her lovely blue eyes that remind him of bottomless clear blue lakes. His thumb gently smoothes the tears away and his heart breaks at Dianna's tremulous attempt at a smile. "I'll go have a word with Sister and see if she'll let me take you home now. But if it has to be later, at least you'll know it will be today," he assures her, and places a kiss on her forehead before rising.

Explaining the situation to the Ward Sister, Lucas isn't disappointed when she asks him to wait for a doctor to approve the discharge.

"We have already got a preliminary indication that Mrs Linden will be discharged today. There were no complications and her observations have been good overnight," the Sister tells him. "We're expecting a doctor at around 8 a.m., if you want to wait with Mrs Linden until then that's fine, as long as you're quiet."

Taking the woman's face between his hands, Lucas gives her a smacker of a kiss – much to the other nurses' delight.

"Well I never..." the Sister gasps, then blushes wildly and waves him away.

The two hour wait doesn't take long to pass and when the doctor agrees to the early discharge, both Dianna and Lucas are overjoyed.

Dressed in a hospital nightdress and theatre gown, Dianna is wheeled to Lucas' car and lifted into the passenger seat.

"I'm going to send that Sister a nice big bunch of flowers," Lucas smiles up at Dianna as he snaps her seatbelt in place.

"All the nurses were very kind," Dianna tells him.

"Then I'll think of something they can all share," Lucas nods to confirm his thoughts. "But let's get you home; I know Helen and Bill will be pleased to see you."

But Dianna frowns, only now thinking of the burden she will be to the kindly housekeeper.

"Will you stop worrying," Lucas tells her when he sees the giveaway frown. "Helen will love having you back...and so will I," he adds, and reaches over to give her hand a reassuring squeeze.

Sure enough, Helen and Bill are there to greet her when Lucas pulls the car up at the main door.

Rounding the car, Lucas scoops Dianna up into his arms and carries her into the house.

"You look a little peaky..." Nurse Baxter observes as Lucas carries her patient up the stairs to her old bedroom. "We'll get you settled in and then I'll take your observations and we'll go from there."

Never has Dianna been so glad to see a bedroom or the people who are in it. She has friends who truly care about her, and she is so grateful for them.

"With your permission, Bill will take me to your cottage to get you a few essentials," Helen tells Dianna with a smile. "I'll let Gillian take care of you just now."

When the room empties and Dianna is left alone with Nurse Baxter, she asks a question that has been needling her, "I just wondered...," she begins hesitantly, "...that day when you and Helen were...err...disagreeing about my trip into the garden... Well, you both looked ready to do battle, yet the next time I saw you...well, you seemed like best buddies," she finishes with a nervous chuckle.

Straightening Dianna's bedding, Nurse Baxter nods her head and smiles, "I remember. But it wasn't really a disagreement, just a difference of opinion," she explains tactfully. "And not even that; once we expressed our concerns it was clear that we both had your best interests at heart and that was that."

"Well, I'm glad you could come back," Dianna sighs, tired now that she is settled into bed. "I did wonder if you would want to."

But Dianna doesn't hear Nurse Baxter's reply, as she falls fast asleep in the comfy bed.

CHAPTER ELEVEN

"Will you have time to handle the Broadbent visitors?" Lucas asks Hank from his downstairs home office.

"No problem. There's nothing on today that needs your immediate input. And by the sounds of things, you're needed more at home," Hank sighs, sad to learn that Dianna has lost her baby. "Life's a real bitch sometimes," he observes in his deep growl of a voice. "A real damn bitch."

"I can't disagree," Lucas tells his longtime friend. "If you're really sure, I'll be in first thing tomorrow."

Life's a bitch, alright. But at least I have some good friends to rely on; Dianna has no one. Well, from now on she'll have me!

Later that morning, Helen answers a call from Dr Alex

Harvey, concerned about Dianna and asking when it would be convenient for him to visit with her.

"What do I tell him?" she asks Lucas after explaining the situation.

"You could tell him to go to hell," Lucas snaps out angrily, then smiles darkly. "Or you could just put him through to me and let me do it?"

Looking doubtful about that idea, Helen says, "I could just tell him that Dianna isn't up to visitors yet?"

Pursing his lips at her, Lucas pulls a comical face and says, "If you must. But if he calls again just put him straight through to me."

The damn man doesn't know when he isn't wanted! But I'll soon put him straight on that! There's something about him that doesn't sit well. He's too charming, too damned polite on the surface...but I don't think it goes more than skin deep. I'll try to find out more from Dianna. But I need to keep it light or she'll suspect something and probably clam up.

She kept her secret about Davey for years without anyone guessing the truth. If Harvey is wheedling his way into her life when he isn't wanted... Well, I'll think about the consequences when I know more.

If there's one thing that Lucas can't stand it's pushy people, or bullies. And the two were one and the same in some circumstances.

He's been lucky in his life, Lucas is aware of that. But he has never revelled in it, never lorded it over his workers or friends.

He treats people as his equals; he needs the skills of the people who work for him just as much as they need the pay packet he gives them at the end of the month. And he hopes he is a good employer; he certainly sets out to be.

But Lucas is no pushover, he knows how to play boss with a worker who is trying to take the piss. He doesn't stand for shirkers, work place bullies or trouble makers, and Hank is too good at managing the workforce to allow it to go unnoticed.

If a man, or woman, does a fair days work he pays them more than the average wage in return.

Most people like working at the quarry — and soon it will be able to offer more work to the local community. And a lot of that will be down to Dianna, the way she stood up for him at the Planning Hearing.

I don't know how she did that. All those people listening to the details of her private hell — I would never have put her through that willingly. But she is one hell of a woman. Her courage is boundless — but that doesn't mean it didn't hurt to do it.

I'm just glad those people showed her how proud of

her they were, and not just because she stood up for the quarry expansion that would provide work for their sons and daughters. They were proud of her as a woman, as someone who's come out the other side of a nightmare and is the better for it!

I know I was. Am. Dianna is one in a million and I want her in my life...forever. I just have to figure out how...

At lunch time, Lucas asks Helen to serve his meal with Dianna's in her bedroom and plans to put a small table and a couple of chairs on the balcony so that they can enjoy the lovely day.

Working in his office for a couple of hours to give Nurse Baxter time to settle Dianna in and do any necessary cares, Lucas finds himself lost in thought rather than working.

Standing at the window he surveys his garden and watches Jimmy at work.

How did Dianna's life come to this, battered and bruised on a regular basis, then almost losing her life and the baby she was carrying?

And all at the hands of a man who professed to love her! What a joke! If that's any man's idea of love it's them who needs counselling and their balls handed to them on a bloody plate!

Knowing that he isn't going to be able to do any work

while he's thinking about Dianna, Lucas goes up to her room and knocks gently on the door.

Nurse Baxter answers and puts a finger to her lips while opening the door wider to let him in.

"Mrs Linden has been asleep almost since she got here," the nurse tells him. "She must have had a bad night so I'm happy to leave her and wait for her to wake on her own."

Nodding, Lucas crosses the room to stand at the end of the bed and is worried to see Dianna looking so frail and pale, lost in the large bed.

"She's lost weight. I don't think she can have been eating properly even before this happened," he observes quietly.

"I would agree..." the nurse moves closer to his side and puts a comforting hand on his arm, "...but we'll make sure Mrs Linden gets her strength back and takes the time to heal fully – body, heart and mind."

"Do you know the names of any good counsellors?" Lucas asks, turning to the nurse.

"I don't know how you'd feel about it, but I'm a trained counsellor; I've taken many courses over the years and do private counselling as I can fit it in around my other commitments."

Lucas is surprised and it shows on his handsome face.

"You really are a remarkable woman."

"Well, I've always had an interest in people, more than just the physical, if you see what I mean?" Nurse Baxter explains. "When I worked in a hospital I saw many people, young and old, who'd reached their breaking point and taken an overdose or tried to end their lives in other ways. That's when I started to take the counselling courses and did some work for the Samaritans."

"If you can help Dianna by talking her through this mess, then by all means do it," Lucas looks back at the slight woman in the bed. "I'll gladly double your wages to stay on and get Dianna through this. She went home too soon, in my opinion. Though I'm not sure why – Dianna appeared to be happy and settled here, then she wasn't," he frowns, trying to recall what might have happened to change that, but fails to think of anything.

"I'll gladly stay on as long as Mrs Linden needs me," Nurse Baxter smiles. "But as to doubling my wages, there'll be no need for that."

"Hmm..." Lucas is lost in thought, still musing over Dianna's sudden need for independence and her insistence that she move back to her cottage.

There's something not quite right. I was too stunned to really think about it before, but there was definitely something at the back of Dianna's sudden decision to move back home...but what?

Leaving Dianna to sleep, Lucas goes down to the kitchen and sits at the kitchen table, watching Helen prepare lunch.

"How is Dianna?" Helen asks, knowing that Lucas has just come from seeing her.

"Sleeping," he tells her. "I hope you've got something really fattening in mind for lunch – I don't like to see how thin Dianna has become." Then he frowns and asks an entirely different question, "Do you have any idea why Dianna left so suddenly before? I mean, the more I think about it the more strange it feels. Dianna was happy here, wasn't she?"

Looking a little shame face, Helen decides to admit something she isn't proud of. "I did hear something," she begins tentatively. "I'd like to say it was accidental..." and she winces with the shame she feels at listening in on someone else's private conversation, "...but it wasn't. I was concerned for Dianna," Helen suddenly stills her hands and glares at Lucas defensively, her voice going louder with her growing agitation. "I didn't trust that man...I had a feeling he was influencing Dianna to do things the way he wanted them done. And I was right," she finishes with a firm nod of her head.

Raising a brow in surprise, Lucas holds a hand up to call a halt to his housekeeper's uncharacteristic rant.

"I understand that you were looking out for Dianna," Lucas placates quietly. "But now I need you to tell me what you overheard and why you were so concerned in the first place."

"I'll make some tea," Helen tells him, turning to switch the kettle on. "I talk better over a cuppa."

Minutes later, when they are both settled at the kitchen table, a mug of tea between their hands, Helen tells Lucas what she knows and what she suspects.

"It was little things, at first," she begins. "Dr Harvey appeared kind and caring on the surface but I was beginning to see another side to him."

"Did you see him do anything inappropriate to Dianna?" Lucas asks, his hands now squeezing the mug sat between them.

"Not exactly..." Helen considers, "...it was more a shift in his ways. At first I thought, what a lovely man to take time out from his busy life to look in on one of his old patients. But the more I saw of him the more I saw through him." With her eyes lowered to the table, Helen finds it difficult to continue.

"I need you to be completely honest with me if we're going to help Dianna," Lucas tells her, and waits for Helen to look at him. "Now tell me everything; what you thought, what you felt, what you saw and heard...everything, Helen."

Nodding, Helen takes a couple of sips of tea then sighs heavily. "I started to notice that Dianna would start off smiling when Dr Harvey arrived, but before long the smile would vanish and I started to wonder why. I mean, if it had been just the once then I wouldn't have bothered. But it got so as it would be every time, and that's when I decided to listen in," she confesses.

"It's not like he was being an outright bully, but some of his opinions were a bit strong and when Dianna tried to disagree or make her own opinions known, he didn't seem to like it," Helen finishes, feeling guilty for having listened in, and now even more guilty for not telling her boss at the time.

"I see," Lucas considers, sipping at his tea and mulling over what he's been told. "Do you think he was the one behind Dianna's move back to the cottage?"

Nodding, Helen looks at her employer with concerned eyes, "I do. In fact, I heard him tell her that she needed to move on, get her independence back and start living her own life instead of relying on others to take care of her." Sighing again, Helen remembers the look on Dianna's pale face when Dr Harvey had all but accused her of malingering and taking advantage of the people around her.

"He said that, did he?" Lucas growls quietly,

dangerously. "I knew there was something about that man I didn't like. The next time he calls you put him straight through to me. Right...?"

"I will, yes," Helen replies, a heavy burden of guilt lifting off her now that she has told Lucas everything.

Sitting on his own in his office, Lucas mulls over the problem of Dr Alex Harvey and decides he bears a closer look. Maybe he has prior form for this type of behaviour – latches on to a vulnerable, attractive patient then gives her a follow up call as a friend. She's been discharged so no outward conflict of interest evident – I don't imagine he makes a move on them while they're still in the hospital.

But once they are back home...

Yes, Mr Harvey, I think you bear much closer scrutiny, and if I find out you've done this kind of thing before I'll be gunning for you!

Bill is helping Jimmy out in the garden, the two men digging a plot of ground over ready to replant it.

When he hears his name called, Bill looks back to the house and the kitchen window, where he sees Helen waving for him to come in.

"Be back in a mo," he tells Jimmy, planting his spade in the turned earth.

"No rush, you take your time," Jimmy replies, his

north Yorkshire accent not thinned out for all the 20 years he's been living in Ireton.

Crossing the garden, Bill tidies a few things as he goes along. A couple of plant-pots left from an earlier planting session and a trowel laid next to them.

Before he goes indoors, Bill takes a look around the garden and feels a glow of satisfaction at the bright blooms and neatly trimmed lawns.

Not officially a gardener, he does a bit of this and a bit of that as needed. He and his wife have lived at the house since Lucas' father had bought it, back before Lucas had even been born.

They hadn't been blessed with their own children, but Bill and Helen hand enjoyed taking care of Lucas and hoped they would be around to take care of the next generation too.

"What is it, woman?" Bill asks his wife in mock annoyance. "Can't you see we're up to our armpits in planting?"

Pointing at his feet, Helen tells Bill to stay exactly where he is, "Don't you dare tread that mud into the house. I've scrubbed this kitchen floor and I won't have you traipsing those filthy boots all over it!"

Not that he would, and Helen knew it, she was just being cautious and still feeling a little sensitive after her admissions to Lucas.

Heeling off his boots, Bill stands them outside the back door then moves across the kitchen to give Helen a peck on the cheek. "You're lovely when you're angry..." he teases, "...have you and Nurse Baxter had a spat?"

"Not at all, Bill Layton!" Helen puts her shoulders back and tilts her chin up, "Gillian is a fine nurse, we may have had our differences in the past, but I'm very glad Lucas was able to get her back for Dianna's sake."

"Alright..." Bill purses his lips then smiles when he notices that lunch is ready, "...ahh, you called me in for lunch. That looks right tasty," he tells her, crossing to the sink to wash his hands.

"When you've finished cleaning yourself up, you need to go to Lucas' office and give him a knock. He wants you to help him get a small table and a couple of chairs out on Dianna's balcony so that they can eat lunch together," Helen informs him, and watches as her husband's face falls in disappointment.

"Oh. Right then," he mumbles, drying his large hands off. "I'll get to it."

But before Bill can exit the kitchen Helen gives him a call and takes a plate out of the oven, "This is for you...when you've finished helping Lucas."

With his eyes alight and a broad smile back on his lips, Bill blows his wife a kiss and crosses the hall to knock on Lucas' office door.

Putting his head inside, Bill waits for Lucas to finish his call as his boss crooks a finger at him to come in. "Helen said you need a hand rearranging some furniture in Dianna's room?"

Frowning in confusion, Lucas takes a moment to remember his plans. "Yes, yes, that's right. Just a small table and a couple of chairs," Lucas chuckles at his own befuddlement. "Sorry, just been through some complicated schedules for getting the quarry expansion underway; my brains in a spin from all the facts and figures we're having to put together."

"Going well then, is it?" Bill asks as they mount the stairs.

"It's going very well. In a couple of weeks we'll start setting on more workers; that'll mean more catering staff as well," Lucas informs him happily. "We need to provide good facilities to keep our workforce well fed and watered."

"Sounds like a few of our lads and lasses will be finding work very soon," Bill nods, glad to see and feel the positive vibes that his boss is giving off.

"That they will," Lucas claps Bill on his broad back and gives him a mile wide grin as he knocks on Dianna's door and opens it on her invitation. "We did it, Bill. And some of that is down to our lovely guest, the very courageous Dianna Linden."

Sitting on the chaise, Dianna lifts a brow at being called courageous, "What did I do to earn such plaudits?" she asks on a nervous chuckle.

"You helped get the planning consent I needed for the quarry, and I was just telling Bill that I'll be setting on new workers very soon," Lucas smiles brightly.

"Oh, that's wonderful news," Dianna smiles up at him, her heart turning over and her stomach clenching to see his handsome face so happy.

"If you wouldn't mind some company for lunch, I thought Bill could help me get a table and a couple of chairs out onto the balcony?" Lucas suggests hopefully.

"What a lovely idea," and she watches the two men arrange the furniture without much trouble.

"Would madam allow me to escort you to lunch?" he asks, holding his elbow out for her to put her arm through it.

Giggling shyly, Dianna gets to her feet to do so.

Stepping behind her, Lucas holds out her seat then moves it under her as she sits.

Lips quivering with stifled laughter, Dianna watches as Lucas takes his seat and returns her grin across the table.

Shifting a little uncomfortably, she can't imagine what he can be thinking when he looks at her that way. Like she's the very reason he is happy, the simple joy in his life that he can't take his eyes off of.

And he has such attractive eyes, Dianna notices, and feels a new warmth fluttering through her body as she looks into them.

His mouth looks soft and full, and the smile melts as her eyes continue to take in the sensuous quality of it. It had felt good on hers she remembers, and unconsciously she raises a finger to touch where his mouth had been, and her lips part on a sigh.

"I've done you steak and salad with a few new potatoes," Helen tells them as she steps out onto the balcony and places a plate in front of Dianna. Turning, she takes another plate from Bill and places it in front of Lucas. "Enjoy it while it's hot and I've got a lovely pudding for afters," she smiles, happily unaware that she has shattered a magical moment.

"I didn't know if you'd want wine with that?" Helen turns quizzical eyes to Lucas. "Or I could bring some tea or coffee up if you'd prefer?"

"Just tea for me please," Dianna smiles up at Helen, glad for the distraction. Where was my mind going a minute ago – I hope Lucas didn't notice. It was just the way he was looking at me. No one's ever looked at me that way...like I'm exactly right...exactly the person they want to be with...

Giving herself a mental shake, Dianna realises that

they are alone again and concentrates on her meal.

"What were you thinking about, just now before Helen arrived?" Lucas asks, his grey eyes narrowed and watching her closely.

Feeling her cheeks heat, Dianna lowers her head over her plate and carefully cuts up her steak. "I can't remember," she shrugs, hoping it looks casual.

But Lucas' mouth pulls into a slow smile that would tell her that he knows exactly what she was thinking, if only she had the courage to look up. "Liar."

Lifting her head with a denial on her lips, Dianna catches the glint in his eyes and knows he's on to her. "Perhaps I was thinking of Alex," she tells him, and watches the gleam turn dark and his soft mouth draw into a hard line. "I'm sorry; I don't know what made me say that. It was stupid."

"Do you think of him often?" Lucas' voice has grown quiet and Dianna wishes she hadn't been so careless.

"I..no..it's just...he's probably worried about where I am," Dianna tells him hurriedly. "I didn't think to call him...when things went so horribly wrong," she finishes sadly.

"No, you didn't did you. Why is that?" he asks, sitting back in his chair to regard her.

Looking confused, Dianna slowly shakes her head and has to wonder at that.

"He's a doctor after all," Lucas persists when Dianna doesn't answer. "I would have thought he would be the first person you would think of in such circumstances — yet you thought of me."

CHAPTER TWELVE

Standing on her balcony later that night, Dianna looks up at an ink black sky covered in stars gleaming like diamonds.

Hugging her arms about her, she tries to admire the beauty of the night, to enjoy the scents wafting up on the gentle breeze that is ruffling her long auburn hair but her senses are alive with other feelings. Feelings Dianna doesn't want to acknowledge or dwell on, but she knows they are there, lurking behind the shadows of her sadness.

"Our baby is gone, Davey," she whispers. "Is that what you wanted...would that have made you happy?"

Amazed that her eyes are dry, Dianna puts a hand to her stomach and feels the pain of grief stab through her. "Why, Davey? Why couldn't you find joy in the prospect of becoming a father? Why did it have to make you angry, to fill you with such horror that you almost killed us both?"

Sitting at the table, still there from the disastrous lunch she had shared with Lucas, Dianna leans back in the chair still looking up to the heavens.

"Was I such a terrible wife? Didn't I ever make you happy?" she asks forlornly. "I tried, Davey. I know I wasn't very good at doing things the way you liked, but I tried. I tried so hard..."

The breeze has turned cold and Dianna feels it to the core and shivers violently. "I wish I could understand what I did to change things – you were such a different person when we first got married."

Getting to her feet, Dianna walks to the balcony doors and takes one last look at the night sky, "I loved you, Davey. I really did." Then she steps back into her bedroom and closes the doors.

Unnoticed by Dianna, Nurse Baxter closes the interlinking door to her bedroom having heard the solitary lament and decides to broach the idea of counselling with Dianna in the morning.

Morning dawns in a rainstorm more suited to winter than the middle of summer, and Dianna listens to it pound against the windows.

Walking to the balcony door, she rests her forehead against the glass and looks up at the dark grey sky. The mood of the weather seems to match her own, and Dianna finds it difficult to pull herself out of the pit of despair she now finds herself in.

"Breakfast is ready, Dianna," Nurse Baxter calls from behind her.

"You go ahead, I'm not hungry," Dianna turns to give the woman a perfunctory smile, but can't manage even that.

"Then come and sit with me and have a cup of tea," Nurse Baxter suggests, though her face and the hand beckoning her over leave Dianna in no doubt that she won't take no for an answer.

Taking the lid off her plate of omelette, mushrooms and grilled tomatoes, Nurse Baxter deliberately wafts the appetising scent over to Dianna.

"Helen always does such a good breakfast; don't let it go to waste," the nurse smiles kindly and is rewarded when Dianna lifts the lid covering her own plate.

Even the thought of Helen's melt-in-the-mouth omelette doesn't get Dianna's appetite stirring, but she gives it a try just to please her companion.

"Dianna, have you ever thought of talking through your recent problems with anyone?" Nurse Baxter queries, still tucking into her breakfast like she's just asked Dianna to pass the salt instead of something as deep and meaningful as 'have you ever thought of counselling'. But she has been careful not to use that word; it often gives people the wrong idea and puts them off seeking help.

"I've thought about it..." Dianna admits cautiously, "...but the idea of going to a stranger's office to talk about my private life isn't very appealing."

Nodding wisely, Nurse Baxter looks up at the young woman sitting opposite and feels her heart twist at the trials she has been through. But her voice betrays none of that when she says, "You could always talk to me."

Looking taken aback, Dianna can only stare at the nurse she has come to trust. "You...?"

"Yes. But only if you feel comfortable with that idea," the nurse tells her. "I assure you, nothing you might say to me would go any further. Nothing," she repeats when a glimmer of doubt enters Dianna's eyes.

"Not even to Lucas?" she asks, knowing that it is he who is paying the nurse's wages.

"What we discuss is strictly between you and I; that goes for anything we have ever discussed," the nurse emphasises. "Confidentiality is at the heart of what we nurses do; you need have no fears on that score."

Hesitating only a moment, Dianna begins to tell the nurse all about Davey. Not just the horrors of the later years of their relationship, but the joy of their wonderful beginning.

"He was so funny..." she chuckles, not realising that her mood has already lightened, "...it was a nightmare during our last couple of years at college, he would pull silly faces at me across the room to get my attention."

"Is that when you started courting?"

"That's a lovely word, isn't it? Courting...it reminds me of romance and flowers, the way a man wooed a woman in the olden days of chaperones and chaste kisses," Dianna smiles delighted. "And I suppose that's what Davey did in his own wacky way."

"And how was that?" the nurse asks, giving Dianna just a gentle nudge to continue.

"Oh he'd give me flowers alright..." she smiles brightly, "...only they weren't the kind you bought in any flower shop. He'd pick Dandelions, Daisy's, Buttercups and Bluebells – whatever was about and handy to make me a little posy." Her smile turns wistful with the remembering, "I loved those silly flowers and I know that he liked that I loved them."

"You were young and full of the confidence of youth, but were you in love yet?" Nurse Baxter smiles and raises an inquisitive brow.

"I was getting there fast. Davey was a charmer, and he could have had his pick of the girls – I was always a little stunned that he picked me," Dianna confesses, then realises that she has completely cleared her plate. "Gracious, I must have been hungrier than I thought," and frowns down at her plate in surprise.

"Let's take our tea out onto the balcony..." Nurse Baxter suggests, "...it's stopped raining and the sun is out again."

Turning, Dianna looks across the room to the window and is surprised to find that the nurse is right. "I thought the rain was set in for the day."

Settling themselves on the balcony, the two women are surprised by the heat of the day now that the sun has broken through.

"Isn't it lovely?" Dianna smiles, enjoying the view over the beautifully kept garden. "It's so much larger than you realise on the ground."

"Did you have a garden at the cottage?" the nurse asks.

"We did. Not much of one, and only out the back, but I always put hanging baskets on the front and there's a climbing rose that looks beautiful in the summer," Dianna recalls. "You can't call it a front garden, but there is a sort of small border that I plant right along the front of the cottage."

"Sounds idyllic."

"Yes, that's what I thought when I first laid eyes on it," Dianna's blue eyes go distant with remembering. "It was a day just like this when we first went to look at it. We were so excited...our first home together."

"Were you both born in Ireton?"

"Yes, though Davey lost his parents just before we met and had to move in with a cousin. He doesn't really have any close living relatives."

Not realising that she has slipped back into the present tense, Nurse Baxter decides not to correct Dianna and allows her to continue her tale uninterrupted.

"We sort of knew each other from round and abouts - at a distance, if you see what I mean," Dianna clarifies still dreamy with remembering. "I thought he was gorgeous even then, we just didn't hang in the same circles."

"And your parents, are they still living in Ireton?"

"No, they moved to Derbyshire – dad's health was getting worse and mum couldn't manage the house and gardens like she used to. They live in warden controlled housing now so that they always have someone on hand should they need them."

"My mother loved her garden; I know she misses tending one, though she says their gardener lets her lend a hand now and then," Dianna smiles. "It was a huge step for them to move away, they were born and bred here and loved the village atmosphere and the sense of community that Ireton still has today."

Looking down over the balcony, Dianna can see Bill and Jimmy finishing off the planting of the freshly dug area they've been working on. Jimmy must be in his forties and Bill looks to be a little older, but both men look fit as a fiddle to Dianna's eyes.

"This is a beautiful home," Dianna says suddenly off topic. "Being married to Davey has given me Lucas as a new friend and I'll be forever grateful for what he's done for me."

Sensing that their discussion about Davey was over for now, Nurse Baxter suggests a walk in the garden together. "It looks like there's a footpath leading across that field; a little exercise might do you good," she encourages, but doesn't have to push too hard as Dianna turns a smile to her and nods in agreement.

"That sounds wonderful. I'll just change my jumper for a blouse, it really has gotten warm now," Dianna tells the nurse as she gets to her feet.

Dressed in beige linen trousers and dark cream blouse, Dianna heads out for a walk with her nurse.

There is no gate to the field beyond the large rear garden. "I wonder if this is Lucas' land also," Dianna speculates as they make their way along the footpath. "It seems a shame to leave it empty if it is."

"Maybe he has plans for horses or other livestock," Nurse Baxter suggests.

"Nurse Baxter, do you-"

The nurse puts up a hand to stop Dianna and turns to the younger woman with a lopsided smile, "Do you think you could manage to call me Gillian. I feel a zillion years old with you calling me Nurse Baxter all the time."

Letting out a cheerful giggle, Dianna nods agreeably, "I'd like that."

"Now what were you going to ask?"

"Oh, err...oh yes...I was just wondering what your family think about you being away so much. I feel a bit guilty being the cause for it," Dianna admits.

"I don't have much family left," Gillian explains. "I was a young widow and never had any children from the marriage. Always wanted some, but I'm nearing my forties now so I don't imagine that will ever happen."

"I'm sorry." Laying a gentle hand on her companions arm, Dianna really is sorry to learn that this wonderfully caring woman has no one in her life to care about her.

"No matter — I've resigned myself to it, and I love my work," and Gillian smiles sincerely, skillfully masking the shadow of regret.

"I wish I could be so brave – the idea of not being able to have children drives a knife so deep into the heart of me I wonder I don't die from it."

"But that isn't definite," Gillian reminds her.

"No, but I couldn't hold on to this child, why should it be any different if I ever tried again?"

"There are lots of reasons a pregnancy fails," Gillian tries to reassure Dianna. "It doesn't necessarily follow that this one was due to any particular problem you may have. Why, thousands of women every day have miscarriages without ever knowing they were pregnant."

"They do?!"

"Yes, they do," Gillian confirms. "They usually put it down to having a particularly heavy menstrual cycle and put any pain down to severe cramps. They may take a couple of pain tablets to take the edge off and pretty much carry on as usual without any side effects."

"I..I never realised," Dianna frowns down at her flat abdomen and puts a tentative hand to it. "You think it's possible that this was one of those natural miscarriages?"

"I think it's very possible. But many women experience multiple miscarriages before successfully carrying a baby to term," Gillian warns, careful not to raise Dianna's hopes unreasonably. "Then again, some go on to have baby after baby without any further trouble."

Coming to a halt, Gillian smiles over at Dianna with a wise look in her eyes, "Basically, what I'm telling you is that nature is a fickle force that no one can predict. If you look after yourself and it's meant to be then it will be."

"Look after myself...?"

"You've lost a lot of weight, Dianna," the nurse states unequivocally. "Part of what a baby needs is a healthy environment to grow in — that's where taking care of yourself comes in. Eating good nutritious meals, taking regular not too strenuous exercise and trying not to worry are all good things that you can do. Stress can be one of the best contraceptives I know of!"

"I don't understand," Dianna frowns again. "I mean, I understand about the food and the exercise, but how is stress a contraceptive."

"I've found that couples who are so desperate to have a baby and become stressed over it find it very difficult to conceive," Gillian explains. "And many is the time that a couple have given up, decided to move on with their lives only to find that they're pregnant."

"So it was the giving up...the de-stressing, that helped them to conceive?"

"Exactly! The same often happens when a couple go down the adoption route — no sooner have they adopted a child than the wife finds out she's expecting one of their own," Gillian chuckles gaily. "Like I said, nature is a fickle force and we can only go along with what is meant to be. The more we try to take control the more the force of nature is exerted."

Hooking a thumb in the waistband of her trousers, Dianna holds it away from her," I suppose I have lost quite a bit of weight. I'll try to eat healthier and maybe start taking a few slow walks into the village."

"That sounds like a plan," Gillian puts a hand on Dianna's arm and gives it a reassuring rub. "Now I think we've gone far enough for one day, let's head back and sit in the garden for a while."

CHAPTER THIRTEEN

The quarry is buzzing, an air of excitement driving everyone to pull their weight in getting ready for the expansion.

Lucas and Hank are busy organising men and machines as well as filling their order book with new custom.

It feels like the expansion of the quarry and his labour force can't happen soon enough. Fresh orders have been coming in thick and fast, lots of small ones for individual housing projects and some larger ones for garden centres and builder's merchants.

When Lucas begins to ask the customers where they'd heard of his company, quite a few of the new ones said they had a wife, a mother, a sister, or other female relative that attended some women's group or other and that was where the recommendation had come from.

"Cynthia," Lucas grins over at Hank at the end of a particularly busy day. "She not only got the community behind us but she seems to have got the women to spread the word about the quality of stone we provide here."

"Cynthia...how do you know that?" Hank queries, his heavy brows drawn together over dark eyes.

"Because I started asking where the customer had learned of our quarry, and quite a few of them referred to some female relative or other that attends one of Cynthia's groups," Lucas laughs in stunned disbelief.

"Don't go crediting her with an increase in business outside of this office..." Hank warns with a mock frown, "...she'll be putting in a chitty for commission before you know it."

"I think she's just happy that we found work for her son and future daughter-in-law," Lucas grins happily. "How are they working out, by the way?"

"The lad's a hard worker – I've only heard good things about his willingness to help out where needed. And the girl is settling in well. Apparently she tried out a few of Cynthia's recipes in the canteen and they've gone down a storm," Hank smiles and nods his approval.

"Sounds like we got ourselves a bargain pair," Lucas

laughs as he gets to his feet and scoops up his car keys. "Let's hope our new recruits are just as eager. When are you planning on starting the interviews?"

Hank frowns and gets to his feet, joining Lucas at the open office door. "I've had a lot of applicants, some of them from outside of the local pool." When Lucas makes to comment, Hank holds up a staying hand, "I can't prejudice against someone just because they're from a couple of villages over. Work is short all around, but I will give preference to any local applicant who can do the job just as well."

Frowning, Lucas has to agree, "Ok, I can see where you're coming from – but we look out for our own first!"

"Good enough," Hank agrees. "Some of the out of town applicants are from locals who moved away and want the chance to come back. I imagine their parents, or other relatives still living in Ireton have put the word out to them."

"Better and better," Lucas grins. "Don't stay any longer than you have to, tomorrow will be just as busy as today has been," he warns, then steps out of the office and gives his friend a wave as he heads for his car.

When Lucas pulls up on the drive outside of his home he takes a few minutes just to sit and appreciate it.

My father had foresight when he rescued this old

house from crumbling away, and I'm glad he wanted to keep it in the family when he retired.

I hoped to have a child of my own to pass it on to; but I'm beginning to wonder if the right woman will ever come along.

I thought, maybe, Dianna and I were getting close – if only she could let go of her past.

Pushing out of the car and slamming the door shut Lucas strides into the house.

And now I'm starting to think like Dr Smooth-and-slippery! Its Dianna's life, she has to be allowed to make her own decisions. The fact that I love her is by-the-by, it's her...

"Hell, where did that come from?!" Standing at patio doors that lead out to the rear garden, Lucas looks at Dianna sitting with her nurse and smiling happily at their conversation. I don't know why you're so damned surprised, Forrester, you've been falling for her from day one.

Sliding the patio door open, Lucas steps out and walks towards the two distracted women.

"You look like you're enjoying the garden..." Lucas takes a seat to join them, "...it's good to see you looking better."

When Nurse Baxter makes to get up and give them

some privacy Lucas simply smiles and says, "Don't go on my account. We need to enjoy this sun while it lasts, don't we?"

"And I have, but I do have things to do that I've been putting off for long enough," Gillian tells him, and gives Dianna a smile and a nod before leaving.

"Hmm, now I feel like I've chased her away. And you two looked like you were enjoying each other's company," he observes.

"Gillian's been great. We went for a lovely walk over the fields at the back of the garden and I managed to go quite a way," Dianna reports with a happy grin.

"You're on first name terms with the dragon?" he teases lightly.

"Gillian asked me to call her by her given name," Dianna asserts happily. "And she isn't a dragon; Gillian has been very good to me and she listens when I need to talk – but it's nice that she doesn't push when I've had enough."

"Then I'm very happy that she was able to come back and care for you, and I will no longer think of her as 'the dragon'," Lucas grins mischievously.

Looking at the twinkle in his slate grey eyes, Dianna can imagine Lucas as a boy who would get into lots of trouble. "I bet you ran your mother ragged," she giggles over at him. "You have the look of a man who grew up playing tricks on people and falling out of trees that your mother had already told you not to climb."

Eyes wide, and as innocent as he can make them, Lucas says, "What me? I was a good boy, and I only fell out of trees when I was little – by the time I was ten I was too good at climbing trees to fall out of them," he states proudly.

"I hope we didn't trespass on anyone's land earlier," Dianna remembers, not sure whose land they had gone for a walk on.

"No, it's mine," Lucas assures her. "My dad bought it so that no one could build too close to the house, I don't think he ever had any plans for it."

"And you, do you have plans for it?"

"I'm ashamed to say I don't," Lucas actually manages to look shame faced. "I love the gardens as they are, I can't see me expanding them by that much just to make use of the land."

"What about live stock? Maybe you could have horses," she suggests, a wistful look creeping into her lovely blue eyes.

"Do you ride?" Lucas asks, noting that look and wondering at the secrets he has yet to find out about Dianna.

"I did," she states simply, then falls silent for a moment that Lucas deliberately doesn't break. "While you were climbing trees I was riding horses in gymkhanas. My mother was my biggest fan – she kept a small trophy room with all my rosettes pinned to the wall in a special cabinet."

"You were good then," Lucas states, able to imagine her atop a horse quite easily.

"I was," Dianna smiles proudly. "I used to dream of opening my own riding school – you wouldn't believe how far my mother had to drive me to get to the nearest one."

"I never realised that we didn't have one," Lucas frowns, his brain ticking over on the thought.

"No, Ireton has never had one that I know of. The nearest one is two villages over, unless things have changed in the last few years," she speculates.

"No. No, I think I would have heard about it if one had started up," Lucas muses. "I sit on the local Commerce Committee – we try to keep an eye on local businesses to see what is thriving and what might need a helping hand to get through the lean times," he explains.

"What kind of help?" Dianna asks.

"Financial mainly," Lucas replies. "But it could be that they just need help with accounts, planning their incomings and outgoings in a way that will see them through the year more comfortably."

"How do you help them financially – surely you can't afford to just bail businesses out?"

"No, we can't do that, but we can offer loans at considerably less cost than a local bank would charge," Lucas explains.

"I don't understand why you would, though. I mean, what would it matter to you if a few small businesses go under?" she frowns thoughtfully.

"I suppose it has to do with the life of Ireton – either we can nurture it and help it to grow, or we can stand by and watch the life-blood of it ebb away until nothing but the bare bones is left," Lucas explains, his quiet passion unmistakable.

"You love this town," Dianna states just as quietly and with just as much confidence. "That's why you're trying to hold on to our young people, and it's why you're willing to go the extra mile to help struggling businesses." Watching him, she nods in answer to her own thoughts, "I doubt you gain a penny in profit for all the extra work of heading up this 'Commerce Committee'. And you do head it up, don't you?"

Smiling and nodding, Lucas holds his hands up, "Guilty as charged."

He loves this more chatty side of Dianna and doesn't want to let her shut down on him again.

"So what about this riding school idea – are you ever going to do something about it?" he asks, raising a questioning brow.

Blushing at the thought of anyone taking her seriously about business, Dianna shakes her head. "No, Davey was right on that score – I don't know the first thing about business. It was just a childish dream."

His easy smile fades to nothing and his grey eyes darken, "Don't do that. Don't dismiss your dreams on someone else's say so – especially not Davey's!"

"I..I didn't realise that I was," she defends nervously.

Standing, Lucas towers over Dianna then reaches out a hand to help her up. "Come with me," he says, keeping hold of her tiny hand in his.

Wondering where they are going, Dianna manages to keep up with his long strides as they head to where she and Gillian had taken a walk earlier.

"There's four acres of land doing nothing," Lucas states, sweeping his hand in front of them to indicate the surrounding field. "Can't you imagine a stable block and a couple of fenced paddocks? I would think this would be the perfect setting for your riding school, and as local as you can get to the town."

Her mind's eye is imagining herself giving children lessons, watching them progress from beginners to competent riders. I'd have enough room here to set up a competition ring, charge entrants a fee for competing and hold smaller gymkhanas for my students. And maybe I could stable horses for owners, provide food and board and care as their owners decide they need...

Her blue eyes are alive with imaginings and Lucas enjoys watching her envisage it all.

"It doesn't have to remain a dream, Dianna. I could invest in your business, starting small until you get established and then helping you to grow the business until it starts turning a profit."

Looking up at him, Dianna's face is a picture of hope and confusion. "Why?"

"For the same reason I set up the Commerce Committee," Lucas smiles. "This could be a chance to offer our youngsters something that will broaden their horizons. And as there isn't another riding school in the district, it would make good business sense to invest."

"I can't take it all in," Dianna heaves in a breath and lets it out slowly.

"Just take some time to think through what I'm offering," Lucas encourages as they turn to walk back to the house.

A gust of wind blowing across the open field whips Dianna's long auburn hair across her eyes and temporarily blinds her. Stumbling on the uneven ground, she almost falls.

"Hey, steady there..." Lucas shoots out an arm and catches Dianna to him, "...I've got you."

Slightly dazed, Dianna clings to his arms and feels the warmth and strength of them as they hold her for longer than is necessary.

I should be pulling away...shouldn't I? Looking up she can see the fire in his eyes and then can't seem to look away. Without realising, her body has softened against his, is moulding with his the way lovers do. Yes...I should run...I should...

Never breaking eye contact, Lucas lowers his head and claims her mouth with his. Soft, at first, he takes and explores until her eyes close on a groan and her arms go up to twine about his neck.

Now the damn is washed away and the tide of passion flows through them, rushing through their veins and obliterating all reason.

Dianna can feel the hard length of him, their bodies so melded that they could almost be one.

His hands are exploring her, drawing out responses that Dianna can't hold back...doesn't want to hold back...

Crazy...this is crazy...damn these buttons, I need to feel him...

In the end her hands just tug the shirt apart and dive

in to explore the expanse of chest she has secretly admired. She has watched him digging the garden on a hot day, shirtless and tanned, and wondered what it would be like to run her hands over every one of those well-toned muscles.

It has shamed her, made her feel wanton and wet just to look at him, and now she is doing everything she had only ever thought about...longed for...denied herself...

Her dress has buttons to the waist but none of them are fastened now. Defter of finger than Dianna, Lucas has swiftly undone them to get at the prize that lay beneath and now he suckles her breasts greedily.

Moans of pleasure drive him mad, and lowering her to the ground Lucas takes her mouth while his hand trails up Dianna's long legs to cup the raging heat of her. When her hips start to buck with desperate need it is all he can do not to take her right there.

Plunging his fingers into her, Dianna lets out a cry that he smothers with his mouth and swallows with great delight, pleasuring her until her body quakes beneath his and then shudders softly while he holds her to him, loving the storm he has released in her.

Neither of them move, so content are they to be in each other's arms that the place and time is of no consequence.

At last he is holding Dianna in a way that his arms

have ached to do, a way he has imagined in dreams that have been driving him crazy.

"That wasn't fair," Dianna murmurs shyly against the heavy pounding of his heart.

Smiling broadly, Lucas brings his lips down to kiss the top of her head and hugs her more tightly to him.

"There will be time for that," he tells her gently. "When you're ready to be with me fully it won't be in a field with the possibility of being discovered hampering our moves."

As if only then realising that she was half naked in a field, Dianna stiffens in his arms and tries to pull her dress back together, "Oh my god! I didn't realise...didn't think..."

"No..." Lucas's smile is almost cocky, "...you really didn't."

Batting at his chest, Dianna struggles to get out from under him but Lucas is too strong for her.

"Just lay still and let me do you up," he chuckles as her cheeks blush deeply. But he takes his time doing so and can't resist flicking a nipple with his thumb in the process.

Feeling her body shudder and hearing the involuntary gasp of pleasure, he has a hard time forcing himself to complete the task.

If we were in my bedroom right now I'd...

But he pushes those thoughts aside with an iron will and helps Dianna to her feet.

One day...one day soon, please God!

Looking down at his ravaged shirt, Lucas raises his eyes to look at Dianna and enjoys the fact that her eyes are still feasting on his body.

"Am I likely to lose a lot of shirts this way?" he chuckles, and pulls her to him again.

"If you go around seducing women in fields you're just asking for trouble," Dianna smiles into that lovely chest, then does something that makes him shudder right down to his loins.

"Damn it, Dianna," Lucas chokes out after her tongue and teeth have finished with his nipple.

"Cover yourself up then," she giggles, and he is delighted to see this playful side of her.

"It's a little hard with half my buttons scattered on the ground," he smiles sexily. "Some woman just attacked me and almost ripped my clothes off."

"I did didn't I," Dianna admits, biting on her bottom lip and remembering how much she had wanted him.

"Don't start over thinking it," Lucas warns, seeing the doubt creep into her beautiful eyes. "We've been dancing around our feelings for long enough, it's time to start exploring them and see where that leads us."

CHAPTER FOURTEEN

Dianna has to admit, just to herself, that facing up to her feelings for Lucas has been a great relief. Since that day in the field they have been closer on every level, talking for hours and holding hands like a couple of school kids.

They've talked about the riding school, the finance that Dianna could raise against the cottage to match the investment that Lucas is willing to put in. And Dianna begins to realise that her dream could really come true.

"But what if we don't work out?" Dianna expresses her doubts to Gillian before her planned walk into town. "The business could suffer, or even become impossible because of our personal differences."

"If you really think that, you need to discuss it with Lucas before you enter into anything legal," Gillian advises.

Pulling a cardigan over her blue summer dress, Dianna picks up her purse and walks towards the bedroom door.

"I'm probably just trying to find an excuse not to take the plunge," Dianna smiles and shrugs her slender shoulders. "But I will talk to Lucas, just to put my mind at rest.

"Dianna, are you sure you don't want me to come with you?" Gillian asks, concerned that her charge still isn't back to full fitness yet.

"I'll be fine. See you later," she waves and sets off for her first solo walk into the small town centre.

Lucas's drive is quite long and the road running out front of it is winding and slopes gently downhill.

With a breeze lifting her hair, Dianna's heart feels light as a feather and she reaches the town centre in no time at all.

Walking just a little further on the main street, Dianna takes a left turn and enters Sanderson Park – named after Frederick Sanderson, who helped establish the town in the early 19th century.

It was just a small village then, and some of the original buildings are still standing, preserved for posterity. The old Guildhall is now a library and is constantly in use by the community.

At the centre of the park is a small lake; apparently

one of Sanderson's descendants filled it with fish in his honour, though fishing is not allowed.

Today there are families picnicking and feeding the ducks, parents pushing children on the swings and older children working themselves up to touch the clouds on the bigger swings.

What a beautiful day. Dianna sits on a bench watching the children at play in the large sandpit and her heart clutches at the sight of a mother lifting her baby from a pram. Maybe one day...if I'm very careful and very lucky...

Getting to her feet, Dianna realises that she isn't ready for this yet; the pain of losing her baby is still too fresh and raw.

Walking in the opposite direction, she heads for the large pavilion that provides refreshments.

"Dianna, it's good to see you," Alex Harvey steps into view and makes Dianna jump.

Clutching a hand to her heart, she stops, "Good grief, Alex, wherever did you come from?"

"I was just walking along this path and spotted you," he tells her, his eyes narrowing to take in her frail appearance. "You've lost weight, Dianna. Are you sure you're well enough to be out on your own?"

Heaving out a breath, Dianna purses her lips and frowns, "Don't you start on me as well, Alex. I needed some exercise, and this is the first time I've been out on my own."

Holding his hands up with palms out, Alex gestures for peace. "Hold on there, I'm not criticising, just making an observation."

Feeling ashamed of her outburst, Dianna puts a hand to his arm and asks, "How about joining me for a coffee – my treat to make up for my rudeness."

"I'd love to join you for coffee, but it will be my treat as I haven't seen you in quite a while," he smiles winningly, and is pleased when she gives in.

Persuading her to have a scone with her coffee, Alex carries their tray to a more private corner of the large room. Taking her hand he says, "I've missed you, Dianna. I called a few times to find out how you were, but I doubt my messages were passed along."

Not wanting to show her surprise, Dianna lowers her eyes and gently removes her hand to cut her scone in two with rapt attention.

"Lucas has been so kind to me, Alex. I telephoned him in the middle of the night when the miscarriage happened, and he came to my aid immediately," she sighs, then looks up at him when it becomes unavoidable.

"As I would have done had you called me," Alex proclaims. "But you didn't, Dianna. Despite the fact that I am a doctor and could have helped you, you called Forrester instead."

"I...don't know why...," she mumbles uncertainly, suddenly remembering the way Alex had previously begun to make her feel small. "It was just instinct, I suppose. The fact that Lucas took care of me the last time I was ill."

"That's all I've wanted to do for you, Dianna. Take care of you and help you to reclaim your independence," he states softly, but a hint of something else, something not so gentle and comforting is in his voice.

And Dianna hears it and realises that this is why she hadn't called Alex. She is afraid of him.

Never anything but outwardly caring and friendly, she had sensed an undercurrent of something in Alex that reminded her of Davey when he was about to strike out.

"I'm sorry if I upset you, I really didn't mean to," she tells him over the cup of coffee she has to hold steady with two hands.

Then suddenly Alex leans back in his chair and chuckles and the mood lifts. "Don't give it another thought – I'm just being moody because I haven't seen you for such a while. And after you've been ill, too. Are you really alright?"

Grateful for the relief in tension, Dianna nods and

smiles happily. "I really am. It isn't easy seeing all the mothers and babies here, but I'll get over that in time I'm sure."

"Yes...yes you will," Alex nods with conviction. "You're a stronger woman that I would have thought. Good for you."

The next couple of hours are passed comfortably enough, with Alex escorting Dianna around the shops and to the fountain in the town square.

"I've had a lovely time, thank you, Alex," she smiles up at him, sure now that any threat had been imagined. "You've always been good to me, giving up your precious days off to visit me. And now I've taken your time up again, sorry."

"Nothing to be sorry about," he tells her, patting the hand in her lap. "Now let me give you a lift – you look tired and in need of a rest."

I really do feel tired, and it would be silly not to accept a lift...

"That would be lovely," Dianna accepts graciously. "I walked further than I intended."

Doing as Alex suggested, Dianna waits for him to get his car and pick her up from the bench they have been sitting on next to the fountain.

The sun is still out but the air is getting a chill to it and

Dianna rubs her arms to warm them.

"Dianna...," Alex calls out to get her attention.

Getting to her feet, Dianna walks to his car and climbs inside with some relief. "Thank you so much for the lift, I'm not sure I would have made it back in one piece," she smiles over at him and relaxes into her seat.

"It's my pleasure to care for you, Dianna. I have nothing but your best interests at heart," Alex states sincerely.

But when they drive by the hill that leads to Lucas's home, Dianna becomes alarmed. "Alex, you've missed the turn," she tells him, and turns from looking at the road now behind them to stare in shock at Alex.

"It won't take long..." Alex smiles reassuringly, "...I just want to show you my home. I think you will like it – it is very old and I have recently finished restoring it."

"But...I thought you were taking me home," Dianna mutters nervously, and too late realises what she has said.

"Forrester's house is not your home!" Alex bites out angrily. "He keeps you there to make you feel dependant on him, not because he cares for you!"

"I don't understand..."

The alarm she had felt at Alex missing the turn off has now grown into panic. I need to stay calm, talk to him and try to get on his good side. He can't mean to harm me...he's always telling me how much he wants to look after me...

"There is nothing to understand," he tells her, his voice more controlled in a bid to smooth over his angry outburst. "You will like my home, Dianna; I have some beautiful artwork I think you will appreciate."

Calm...stay calm and go along with anything he says...

"I didn't realise you were a collector," she tells him, and forces a smile onto her tight lips.

Pleased by her interest, Alex smiles as though there is nothing at all strange in their situation, "My mother taught me much about art and now I am becoming something of an expert. I have an eclectic taste..." he tells her, and chuckles at the thought, "...my collection covers many eras and styles – I buy what catches my eye, and my eye spots quality with unfailing accuracy."

"That must be an expensive hobby," she observes, hoping to keep the conversation going along on an even keel.

"I am not a poor man," Alex tells her, sitting up straighter in his seat. "Forrester is a pauper by comparison."

"I.I didn't realise," Dianna stutters, taken aback by his proclamation.

"Yes indeed. I could take care of you far better than

Forrester ever could. You would never have to work if you married me," he states, surprising a loud gasp from Dianna.

"Alex, we've never talked about marriage," Dianna exclaims, not able to comprehend where the notion has come from.

"But we would have, if Forrester hadn't kept you away from me," he states confidently.

Pulling his car up outside a pair of wrought iron gates, Alex presses a remote control to open them and drives through and up to an impressively large house.

At any other time Dianna would have admired the lovely architecture and the beautiful gardens surrounding it, but when the gates close behind them she feels nothing but the most disabling fear and dread.

<u>CHAPTER FIFTEEN</u>

"Hi Jimmy, how's it coming?" Lucas asks his gardener who is now starting to plant up the newly dug area that he and Bill have been working on.

"This is the bit I really enjoy," Jimmy smiles happily, his hands covered in soil and fertiliser. "We've got a lot of our own cuttings ready to put in but I've also been to the garden centre to get a few large pieces to give it more structure and texture," the gardener explains."

"Fine, I know I can trust you to do a good job – just charge the account for anything you need," Lucas tells him, and then gives the garden a good look-over. "Is there anything you want me to get my hands into?"

Knowing that his gardener isn't afraid to tell him to leave well alone if needs be, Lucas always confers with his gardener of many years before diving in to help with a job he finds great pleasure in.

"There's some deadheading to do on the east side," Jimmy scratches his chin, considering the jobs he's got listed in his head. "And some of the topiary could do with neatening up. The horse near by the large oak tree looks like it's sprouting wings ready to fly off," Jimmy growls a chuckle.

"Hmm, I usually try to stay on top of the topiary but I've been a bit distracted of late," Lucas admits. "I'll get right on it once I've checked in on Dianna."

"Gillian was saying she isn't back yet," Jimmy tells him, then looks uncomfortable when his boss raises a quizzical brow.

"Gillian..?"

"She was admiring the garden..." Jimmy explains, his discomfort making his reply short and gruff, "...we got talking."

"Ok. So what's this about Dianna not being back — where did she go?" Lucas asks, not so much concerned as curious.

"Took a walk into town. Gillian said she was getting a bit stir-crazy and insisted on going alone," Jimmy tells him, his brows drawn together as he thinks about Gillian's anxiety when she'd come to him earlier.

"Sounds like Dianna is getting her confidence back," Lucas observes, pleased that she is finally feeling ready to meet people on her own terms. Losing the baby has hit her hard, he knows, and this is a big step forward for Dianna. "What time did she go out?"

"That's the problem..." Jimmy hedges, his dark brown eyes looking straight into Lucas', "...Dianna left around 10 this morning and Helen said she hadn't phoned to say she was staying in town for lunch. The women seem to think that's a bit odd for Dianna; that she has always called before."

Feeling his stomach clutch with fear, Lucas just knows that something is wrong. I agree with the women – it isn't like Dianna to leave people wondering, she isn't that inconsiderate. If anything she's always hated putting anyone to any inconvenience, this doesn't add up! Not at all!

To Jimmy he says, "Ok, I'll have a word indoors and if Dianna has still not been in touch I'll drive into town and take a look for her."

Nodding, Jimmy puts a hand on Lucas' arm to stop him before he strides off, "If you want a hand with that just let me know. Two of us would cover more ground more quickly."

"Good man," Lucas nods, grateful for the offer. "I'll let you know what's what as soon as I know."

The clutch in his gut has moved up and around his

heart as Lucas nears the house to seek answers. Davey is dead, so Dianna's safety should be ensured – after all, he had been the one beating her to a pulp when the whim took him.

But this is so out of character for Dianna...

Stepping through the back door into the kitchen, Lucas sees his housekeeper wiping her hands on a towel that she is virtually wringing with worry and discussing something with her husband, Bill.

"Problem...?" he asks, looking at the two so deep in conversation that they haven't noticed him come in.

"I was just saying to Bill that it isn't like Dianna not to get in touch after all this time." Helen turns to Lucas with worry lining her handsome face. "She went out this morning and hasn't phoned anyone – and it's her first time out on her own," Helen frets, her hands still wringing the tea towel. "What if she's taken ill somewhere and can't make it back home? What if her mobile isn't working; no signal or maybe the battery has run out?"

With his wife's voice rising on every word, Bill puts an arm around her shoulders. "Don't worry, pet, Dianna'll be back before you know it. She probably lost track of the time – you women always do when you start walking around the shops," he chuckles, but the worried look he sends to Lucas over Helen's shoulder tells a different tale.

"Perhaps you could come with Jimmy and me to take a look around the town?" Lucas suggests.

"Oh, I could come too, the more the better," Helen says before Bill can reply. Then she is off to let Gillian know that they are all going out and to answer the telephone in case it's Dianna calling.

"Bill, you and Helen take the park, Jimmy and I will split up and take a look around the shops," Lucas tells them. "We'll meet back up at the fountain in an hour – we have each other's mobile numbers, call if you find Dianna or get any news."

The ride into town is short and silent, all of them keeping their worried thoughts to themselves, the atmosphere heavy with it.

Having walked around the park in search of Dianna, Helen suggests to Bill that they try the pavilion in case she is having a cup of tea in there.

But having lucked out in the park they also luck out in finding Dianna in the pavilion. "Excuse me..." Helen speaks to one of the staff behind the cafe's counter, "...do you remember seeing a young woman – she's in her mid-twenties, has long auburn hair that reaches the small of her back and she stands around 5'8" tall. Her name is Dianna Linden," Helen adds in the hope that one of the women might know her.

"Dianna..." a young woman coming in from the back kitchen hears the end of the conversation, "...Dianna Linden – she was in here this morning." The girl grins and gives a wicked wink then sighs dramatically, "Had a stunning bit of eye candy with her too. I certainly wouldn't mind a taste of him."

Bill steps forward at hearing this news and asks for a description of the man. "Was he someone you've seen around - a local maybe?"

But the girl is shaking her head, "No, not a local. I know most of the locals with living in Ireton all my life and working here. But I have seen Dianna with him before; they came here a few weeks ago but I didn't get to talk to her that time either so couldn't get the goss' on him."

"Goss'...?" Bill repeats, frowning with confusion.

"Gossip," the girl laughs. "We girls love to share the goss' on our latest fella."

Feeling very old suddenly, Bill thanks her for her time and steers Helen back outside.

"Her description could be of that Alex Harvey," Helen grimaces with dislike. "But Dianna didn't say she was meeting up with him."

"Maybe it wasn't planned," Bill suggests. "Perhaps we ought to ring Lucas and let him know we've had a sighting of her."

"Yes, you do that while I nip back inside," Helen tells him, and turns back into the pavilion.

When she comes out again, Helen is frowning and looking more worried than ever. "She said Dianna looked happy to be with the man at first, then she saw the man getting a bit agitated and Dianna looked uncomfortable, she thought," Helen tells her husband when he finishes on his mobile. "I just bet it was that Alex Harvey foisting himself on Dianna and telling her what to do, just like before!"

"Lucas agrees," Bill tells her. "Apparently they were seen walking around the shops together – some said Dianna was happy and smiling while others said they thought she looked nervy, but put it down to the fact that she's just lost a baby. Understandable," he adds when Helen sighs and shakes her head.

"I suppose, now let's get back to the fountain and hope that Lucas and Jimmy have come across them somewhere," Helen blows out a breath as she hooks her arm into Bill's.

But when they reach the fountain only Lucas and Jimmy are there; no sign of either Dianna or Dr Alex Harvey.

"Sheila Fergusson in the bakery says she saw Dianna getting into a fancy black car – it sounds like Harvey's,"

Lucas states with a look at Helen and Bill that is very telling.

"Perhaps we should check Dianna's cottage..." Helen suggests, not willing to think on the dark side yet, "...we don't want to go reporting her missing to the police and then they find her at home."

"I'm not sure that we could report her as missing," Jimmy puts in quietly. "Dianna's an adult, if she wants to go off with a man of her own free will there's nothing anyone can do about it."

"Dianna would not just take off with any man," Helen asserts fiercely. "Not even one she was happy to be with without letting anyone know!"

"Let's just take a look at her cottage," Lucas suggests, holding a hand up to stop the brewing argument. "If Dianna isn't there...well, we'll cross that bridge when we come to it."

But it doesn't look promising as they pull up to the kerb and find the cottage in darkness.

Night has started to draw in and the tension is high in the car. "Stay here, I'll take a look round back and see if she's in."

The walk to the back of the cottage is like an unwelcome trip down memory lane for Lucas. First he had found Dianna on the brink of death on her kitchen floor, and then he had answered her call for help when she had been in the middle of miscarrying her baby.

Both times there had been a lot of blood and a threat to her life; he just hopes that this time it will be different.

Opening the tall back gate, Lucas walks into the back yard and looks for signs of life. But there are none, not even the glimmer of a dimmed light to show that Dianna might be at home. But he gives the back door a hard knock just in case.

After a few tries Lucas gives up and goes back to join the house staff in his car.

"Nothing," he states, climbing in behind the wheel. "Just give me a minute to check in with Nurse Baxter and then we'll decide what to do next."

But the nurse hasn't heard anything from Dianna, or anyone else for that matter.

Turning in his seat, Lucas looks from one to the other of his companions and asks, "What do you think, is it time to go to the police?"

A definite chorus of 'yes' comes from all around him. "Right then, here goes," and he turns the car around and heads for the police station.

All of them are silent when Lucas finally pulls up on his own drive and they enter the house. Nurse Baxter greets them with worried eyes and looks round them in search of Dianna. "You didn't find her?" she asks, hoping against hope that between Lucas' last phone call and them coming home they had come across her charge. "I knew I should have gone with her – I should have insisted," Gillian cries, putting a trembling hand up to her mouth.

"Now then..." Jimmy moves to her side and puts a comforting arm about the nurses shoulders, "...we all thought it was a positive thing, her wanting to get out on her own. And it still might be..." he encourages, not really believing it to be true, "...Dianna could be off visiting someone and lost track of time. It's possible," Jimmy affirms when all around him turn dubious looks his way.

"If Dianna isn't back by 9 o'clock we'll go out again," Lucas says, looking at the two men.

Time seems to stand still, the hours till 9 o'clock dragging unbearably. But when eventually the designated hour arrives with no word from Dianna, the three men are up on their feet and heading out to search again.

If tea were alcoholic the two women left behind would be drunk and stupefied by now, instead of taking it in turns to pace about the kitchen looking for things to do.

"What do you think, Gillian..." Helen asks again, "...do you think I should call Bill to find out what's going on?"

And again Gillian tells her, "Perhaps best to wait for him, or one of the others, to call. We don't want to distract them."

But it isn't just a lack of patience that has Helen fraught with worry; she fears for Dianna. Dr Alex Harvey had been all sweetness and light on the surface, but she had seen and heard another side to him, one that didn't quell her fear or inspire her trust.

"Mark my words, there's something very wrong going on here," Helen stops her pacing to look over at Gillian. "And I'd bet a month's pay that that doctor is behind it."

"I'm sure Dr Harvey is nothing of the sort," Gillian protests, defensive of someone whose work is closely associated with her own profession. "He has only ever been kind to Dianna and I'm sure, if she is with him, the good doctor will look after her. In fact..." the nurse bristles, sitting up straighter on her chair, "...I wouldn't be surprised if they were enjoying a romantic interlude. You can tell he cares a great deal for her and Dianna always seemed pleased to see him when he visited."

"Hmm, not towards the end," Helen informs her. "I heard the way he was bossing her about, telling Dianna to pull herself together and get on with life. He all but told her she was malingering and taking advantage of those around her − though not in those exact words," the housekeeper admits.

Frowning into another cup of tea, Gillian takes a few considering sips then says, "Maybe he was just trying to encourage Dianna to try to move on."

"It was more than that," Helen insists. "I heard him, he has this tone that brooks no argument, and you know how vulnerable Dianna is. You know about her past with her abusive husband."

"But why would Dr Harvey do anything untoward?" Gillian frowns in contemplation. "I just don't see it, Helen." But she tries to cast her mind back to the young doctor's visits to see if she can remember anything suspect in his behaviour.

He has always been quite charming in her presence, and Dianna has never mentioned being intimidated by him.

But would she? She's only just starting to open up about her husband – what if Helen is right and I've missed all the signs? That would make it my fault – not only did I not go with Dianna into town, I may have given someone the opportunity to do her harm! Oh no...

"Do you really think Dianna is in danger?" Gillian asks Helen, her face ashen and distressed.

Seeing the nurse's changed demeanour and suspecting the reason for it, Helen tries to reassure the woman, "I'm sure Lucas will find her, or will know where Dianna is staying by the time they come home. She may even have decided to stay over with friends."

"But you know as well as I do, Dianna isn't a

thoughtless woman. She would no more stay out overnight without letting someone know her plans than you or I would," Gillian states, her voice not as strong and sure as it usually is.

Not able to contradict her, Helen puts the kettle on again and makes a fresh pot of tea.

CHAPTER SIXTEEN

Feeling groggy and disoriented, Dianna opens her eyes and can't think clearly enough to assess her situation. She only knows that she is frightened, that someone has drugged her and...

Going under again, Dianna can do nothing to save herself from her captor. Alex Harvey now has her exactly where he wants her, reliant upon him and what he decides to provide.

Far from hiding, Alex goes to work and is at his caring best. His heart is full and life can't get much better for this charming medic who has a radiant smile for everyone.

I have what every man wants – especially Lucas Forrester. And now Dianna will see what it's like to be looked after by a real man, a man of taste and fortune who can give her anything her beautiful heart desires, as long it is what I want to give and she earns that privilege.

She'll soon realise and be grateful that I rescued her from the boring, mundane existence she might have had with that loser. In fact, I'll pick her something nice up on the way home.

Having spent the night on his laptop, Lucas Forester has put together a glowing outline of Dr Alex Harvey's illustrious medical career thus far.

Born of a wealthy family and a long line of doctors and surgeons, Harvey appears to be making his ancestors proud with his achievements.

I don't know what to do. The police may have taken down the details but they're not interested in doing anything. And why would they – Dianna's a grown woman; she can make her mind up to go anywhere she chooses at any time she likes.

But I don't believe that's what happened. Trouble is I can't find a shred of evidence to prove otherwise. Even the people we spoke to who saw her with Harvey said she appeared to be happy in his company, and certainly not under any duress.

I think that situation changed when she got into his car; Harvey has to have taken her somewhere!

It is only a little after six a.m. but Lucas is set on a course of action that will involve his good buddy, Hank.

"Yo," Hank sits up in bed to answer his mobile.

"It's Lucas, I need to talk," he tells his friend without preamble. "Dianna's missing; I need your help, Hank."

The news has Hank wide awake and swinging out of bed. "Come over; I'll get the kettle on."

By the time Lucas arrives, Hank has not only made two mugs of coffee but also put together a batch of grilled bacon and scrambled eggs.

"Just give me a minute to plate this up...," Hank tells his friend as he takes a seat at the kitchen table, "...then we can talk and eat at the same time."

A moment later Hank sets two plates on the table, both heaped with food, and takes a seat opposite Lucas. "Ok, let's hear it from the top."

Telling Hank everything, from the suspicions he has about Alex Harvey and what Helen told him about the things she'd overheard, right up to what they now know happened on the day Dianna went missing, Lucas speaks his worst fears out loud for the first time.

"I hate feeling this useless," Lucas admits, and puts his knife and fork down on a plate that is surprisingly empty. "The police don't even seem concerned – I had to stand over them to make sure they filled out the damn paperwork!"

"Looking at it from their point of view..." Hank says,

even though his friend's angry grey eyes are now slicing him to pieces, "...Dianna is free to go wherever she chooses and isn't obligated to let you know her plans." Then he holds up a hand to ward off the tirade he can see waiting to spew off of his friend's tight lips, "Having said that, I'm with you in that this guy sounds more than a little weird. He seems to be some kind of a Jekyll and Hyde character – I'll get my cousin, Marty, to do some checking up on him."

"That's right, I forgot about him being in the police force," Lucas picks up his mug of coffee and takes a good glug to wash the breakfast, and his temper, down. "Do you think he'll be able to do it today? I'm seriously worried for Dianna's safety."

Nodding, Hank gets to his feet and clears away the pots into the sink. "I'll impress that fact upon him and make sure he does if it's at all possible. Marty's a good sort and he hates any kind of domestic abuse – though this sounds like it has the possibility to be much more," he thinks out loud, then turns to find Lucas wide eyed and pale. "Sorry. Sorry, I didn't mean to say it like that."

"No, you're right. But he's rich as hell and the police are reluctant to act because his father is some bigwig surgeon who could cause trouble if they go accusing his son of kidnapping," Lucas sneers, his anger shooting to the surface again.

Money, Lucas has plenty of it — not as much as Harvey evidently has, but it is enough to see him comfortable for the rest of his life if he isn't irresponsible. But Harvey was born into money, had inherited more and is now rolling in it, and that makes the authorities wary of going up against him without some kind of evidence to back them up.

"Is that really what you think happened?" Hank asks, frowning over the dishes he is now running hot water over.

"Don't you...?" Lucas asks, stunned. "After everything I've told you, don't you think he's forced her into staying at his house with him?"

"I know that's what you think, but we have to look at other possibilities too," Hank says, knowing that it isn't what his friend wants to hear. "What if Dianna is taking a time out from everything — just wants some time on her own to come to terms with all the shit that's happened. Losing her husband, bastard though he was, can't have been easy and it's a lot to get your head round."

"But she was happy at the house the last time we spoke," Lucas insists. "There was no reason for her to take off and Nurse Baxter has been helping Dianna to get to grips with what's been going on in her life. It just doesn't make sense."

"Ok, what do you want us to do now?" Hank asks, not

sure that there is anything to be done as things stand.

Putting his head in his hands, Lucas almost despairs, then rubs his face roughly as if to eradicate it. "I want you to take care of the quarry; contact me as you need to but on my mobile only." Lucas stops, consolidates his thoughts and continues, "I'm going to be tailing Harvey. I'm going to watch his every move and see if I can get a look at Dianna at his home."

"Just don't do anything stupid – you'll be no use to Dianna if you're locked up," Hank warns. "Let me contact Marty, see what he comes up with and we'll go from there!"

"I'm not going to do nothing while Dianna's in trouble. But I won't do anything that will get me locked up," Lucas assures his friend when Hank gives him a warning look.

For Dianna the night has passed in a drug induced blur. Her eyes flutter open for the umpteenth time, but still she can't make sense of what she is seeing.

What is this room? Those green curtains...are they curtains...no...no... But no matter how much she tries to focus Dianna can't clear her mind or her vision. Smoothing the flat of her hand over the surface she is laying on, Dianna can feel that something silky is beneath her and something is laying over her. Why can't I think...

Though she manages to stay awake for a while,

Dianna's thoughts are chaotic and abstract. The park, I remember the park...and I think...Yes, I was with someone...but who? Was it Lucas, did Lucas take me to the park? Shopping...no...can't be right. The fountain, I met someone...Gillian? Did Gillian take me to the park?

The chaotic thoughts and the effort of trying to piece them together give Dianna a stupendous headache. Am I dying, is that why I feel so wretched?

Real fear begins to mix with her confusion and Dianna tries to raise her head and move herself. But apart from one hand she isn't able to move anything, not even her head.

My body...all over...lead weight...too heavy...

Falling back into dreams, Dianna is still asleep when Alex arrives home midafternoon. "Come on, sleeping beauty, you can't sleep all day."

As Dianna's eyelids flutter open, she listens to Alex's voice and suddenly becomes filled with fear and stiffens in his supporting arms. "Alex...I don't understand?"

"You took ill while we were out," Alex informs her smoothly. "I brought you back here to look after you. I really think you need to take things a lot slower, you were obviously exhausted after our walk yesterday."

"You...I was out with you?"

"Don't sound so surprised, we often go to the park

together," he tells her, putting a slight spin on the truth. "Let me take a look at you, you're not sounding like yourself – still some confusion and you look very pale."

"Alex, where am I?"

"Home, with me," Alex smiles happily. "Don't you remember me describing my home to you while we had coffee at the park? You said it sounded lovely and that you would love to see it," he lies, but he sounds convincing and Alex can see that Dianna is taking it all in. "After our walk around the shops you waited for me by the fountain in the square, I got the car and picked you up to save you anymore walking."

Frowning down at her, a look of real concern in his eyes, Alex says, "You really don't remember?"

Fighting to think through the pain of the headache, Dianna ruthlessly tugs her vague memories to the fore, "Yes...I remember the fountain, it's...it's coming back to me now."

"Don't give yourself a headache trying to remember details," he distracts her quickly. "Do you want to get up and come downstairs? I have a surprise for you."

His smile is so genuine and his mood so happy, that any doubts Dianna has about Alex seem to dissolve and slip away. "Too late with the headache – my head is throbbing fit to burst," she tells him, and raises a hand to her temple.

"Not to worry, I'll get you something to soothe your head when we get downstairs," Alex assures her.

Then, helping her to swing her legs round to place her feet on the floor in front of her, Alex stands and holds her hands while Dianna struggles unsteadily to her feet.

"This is silly..." she smiles uncertainly, "...I don't remember feeling this way."

"Hmm, I really think we overdid things yesterday," Alex explains. "I did try to tell you that you looked tired after our walk in the park. But you insisted on doing a round of the shops, said you hadn't been able to get out for quite a while and you wanted to enjoy yourself a little more."

There is enough truth in his words to have Dianna believing them. She had felt the need to get out on her own, to feel a sense of independence again. But she can't remember arranging to spend the day with Alex.

"Then I should thank you for indulging me," Dianna smiles sincerely. "But I think I'll take your advice next time and take things a bit slower."

"Good girl," Alex grins, and leans in for a quick kiss. "Now let me give you your surprise," and leading Dianna into the sitting room, Alex makes sure she is settled safely in an armchair before crossing the room to get it.

Pulling up a footstool, Alex sits at the side of her knees

and hands her a velvet covered box in midnight blue. "For you, my darling."

With clumsy fingers that feel like sausages, Dianna manages to open the lid but words completely fail her. "I..I..."

"Diamonds," Alex supplies eagerly. "Nothing less will do for my fiancée."

"F.fiancée...?" she stutters, her blue eyes rise to his, confusion in their depths.

"You really will disappoint me if you tell me you don't remember my proposal," Alex feigns hurt to pull on Dianna's tender heartstrings. "I went down on one knee by the fountain and you said yes - I gave you my grandmothers ring," he says, turning a ring on her finger that she hasn't even realised she is wearing.

Looking at the beautiful diamond ring, Dianna struggles to pull her thoughts together. The fog covering her brain just won't clear. I don't remember. Why don't I remember...?

But the ring is there, no denying it, so it must be true. I am going to marry Alex!

"It is beautiful, thank you Alex." Her voice sounds dull even to her own ears, but Alex looks pleased.

"I'm going to take care of you, Dianna, as you will take care of me," he smiles, though there is an almost demonic twist to it. "I know you will want to perform your wifely duties to the best of your ability, so I will teach you how to behave in the company of my peers; how to be the perfect hostess when we have guests to dinner, and how to please me in every aspect of our lives together."

Even to Dianna's drug addled brain, Alex doesn't sound 'normal'. But the thought soon disappears along with any other doubts after drinking the wine that Alex insists they drink to celebrate.

Just for a moment the bitterness of the wine causes her to grimace. But with Alex's encouragement she finishes it all up 'like a good girl'.

<u>CHAPTER SEVENTEEN</u>

The information that Hank's cousin, Marty, supplies is worrying, to say the least.

"I told you that creep had done this before!" Lucas exclaims as he reads the notes Hank has just handed him. "And they didn't follow up on it then either!"

"No, I asked Marty about that and he said she dropped the charges and wouldn't give a statement," Hank purses his lips and frowns. "They went to follow up after she'd been in to make the initial allegations and her lips were sealed tighter than a Scotsman's wallet. They could see she was scared but they couldn't budge her, and she suddenly came into a windfall of cash," he adds with a raised brow.

"So, he probably threatened her and when that didn't work, or when he wasn't sure that fear alone would keep her quiet, he paid her off," Lucas summarises, and gets a nod of agreement from Hank.

"That's how it plays for me," Hank tells him, and gets to his feet to make the pair of them some coffee.

The office has a decent coffee machine, something both of them had agreed upon since they drank a lot of coffee throughout the day.

Taking a mug over to Lucas' desk, Hank puts it down in front of him and goes back to sitting behind his own desk.

For a moment or two they sit in silence while Lucas reads the notes further. "Christ, this reads like a carbon copy of the way he's been with Dianna. All sweetness and light, nothing is too much trouble, at first; then he starts to get more demanding, wanting things his own way until finally the poor woman was afraid not to do his every bidding," Lucas looks across the office at Hank.

"And did you notice why she was under Dr Jekyll's care in the first place...?" Lucas continues with a sneer in his voice. "No, well let me tell you; she was a victim of domestic abuse just like Dianna. He rides in like a knight to the rescue but then starts his own form of abuse, slowly and not too demanding at first – he doesn't want to frighten them off. But once he's got them where he wants them he's free to push their buttons in any way he chooses. And now he's got Dianna, damn it!" And Lucas' fist pounds his desk so hard his coffee slops over the side of his mug.

"Marty said he'll try to get his bosses to take another look, but he couldn't promise anything," Hank explains. "What did you find out by following him?"

"Nothing really," Lucas admits. "Just that he's a brazen bastard – still went to work like it was a normal bloody day. He's got some brass neck to do that! And I followed him home, so we know where he lives now."

"He's probably been brought up to think he's Teflon coated where the law is concerned," Hank observes cynically. "Marty said there were rumours that daddy had bailed him out of trouble by oiling the wheels of justice to see that his boy didn't get a record – not good when he wanted his son to follow him into medicine, and surgery specifically."

"Why doesn't that surprise me?!"

"An older colleague of my cousins told him about a meeting he'd had with Dr Harvey senior and his wife, a few years ago." Hank leans back in his chair and rocks slowly. "He said the wife didn't say boo, unless it was to ask if they wanted tea or coffee, and even that was after getting her husband's nod of approval. Then she politely excused herself and went to make the tea. He said she was like a lap dog, looking to Dr Harvey for any signal he might give, otherwise she just sat straight backed with her hands folded meekly in her lap."

"So, you're thinking like father like son," Lucas speculates, and gets another nod of agreement from Hank. "They find vulnerable women and mould them to be exactly what they want them to be. The fact that they've been abused over a period of years makes them particularly susceptible to their kind of brain washing."

Finishing off his coffee, Lucas gets to his feet and takes his mug to the little sink. "I wonder if mummy dearest was an abuse victim before she became Mrs Harvey. Maybe the son has been taking lessons from his father?"

Functioning on autopilot, Dianna cooks a basic meal for them both with some assistance from Alex. "Our lives will be full and rewarding if we work together," he tells her across the dining table. "We'll go shopping for new, more suitable clothes for you as soon as you are strong enough," he smiles brightly. "It will be my pleasure to help you pick them out."

"That's very kind," Dianna mumbles agreeably.

"Yes, isn't it?" Alex nods, liking that Dianna is already more compliant. But I might need to reduce the drug dosage; she's quite dull on conversation like this.

The following morning Dianna wakes in the same bedroom she had previously been in, only now her mind is a little clearer.

The more she wakes the more Dianna becomes aware that something is wrong. I don't remember this room or coming to bed, and yesterday is a blur.

Looking down at her left hand she gets the shock of her life, then an obscure memory surfaces. Engaged? Did Lucas propose...did I say yes? Twisting the beautiful diamond ring on her finger Dianna's lips pull into a dreamy smile.

"Nice to see you looking better," Alex makes her start when he appears at the open bedroom door. "Shouldn't you be preparing our breakfast? I have to go to work in an hour."

"Alex!" Dianna's shock can't be hidden, it shakes her to the core and her face pales instantly.

"Well who did you expect," he laughs unkindly. "Now please, don't take too long to come down to the kitchen; I like a cooked breakfast before going in to the hospital."

What's going on, and why is my head so fuzzy? I can barely put two thoughts together...

Getting to her feet, Dianna realises that she is wearing a nightdress that she doesn't recognise and certainly doesn't remember changing into.

Alex...did he put me in this or does he have female staff that got me changed? And what is this?

Holding up a very expensive looking dress Dianna

looks around for clothes she recognises as her own, but there are no other clothes in the room.

Pulling on the underwear that has been set out alongside the dress, Dianna looks at herself in the mirror and barely recognises her reflection. It's like looking at a ghost, her skin is so pale and her eyes look dull and expressionless.

What is happening to me? How did I get here and who am I engaged to?

On entering the kitchen Dianna passes Alex who is reading the Times newspaper at the breakfast table.

"There are eggs and bacon in the fridge," he informs her. "I've put the percolator on as you were late in rising, but would prefer that you undertake that task as part of your duties."

"Duties...?" Dianna asks, even more confused.

"Of course, dearest. Didn't I tell you that I would instruct you on how best to fulfil your role as my wife?" Alex smiles indulgently. "I don't expect you to be perfect, not at first, how could I? You have never mixed with the kind of society that I keep, but you will learn and I will reward you accordingly. You liked the diamond bracelet I bought you," he states with confidence, and his eyes lower to her wrist.

Blinking with surprise, Dianna holds up her arm and

turns her hand to look at the beautiful bracelet. "You gave me this...?"

"Of course, darling. But I don't think you should wear it during the day, it is hardly appropriate adornment for when you are taking care of our home," he chuckles, turning his attention back to the newspaper.

After a moment or two's hesitation, Dianna carries out Alex's request that she cook breakfast. She didn't think she would feel hungry and only got enough out for Alex, but once the bacon starts to cook the lovely aroma gets her stomach rumbling and she adds more for herself.

When did I last eat? How long have I been here? And why can't I remember anything? Did I have a fall and hit my head – it doesn't feel painful.

Questions like these continue to pound against a headache she can't seem to shift.

When Alex notices Dianna rubbing at her temple he asks, "Headache darling?"

"Yes..." she replies as she brings two plates of cooked breakfast over to the table, "...I woke up with it and it doesn't seem to be easing."

Narrowing his eyes at her across the table, Alex decides that Dianna needs a boost of her medication. He doesn't want her to be able to think past anything he tells her; thinking for herself wouldn't do at all.

"I'll take care of that for you," he smiles warmly, his handsome face a picture of concern and adoration. Then he crosses to a locked cabinet and takes out two capsules then locks it up again. "Here you go; these will soon put you back to rights again." And after handing them to her, Alex stands over Dianna to make sure that she takes them. "That's a good girl."

They don't take long to work; Dianna's thoughts no longer feel like her own, they are echoes in a mind that can't quite pull them together enough to question or complain.

"Yes, much better," Alex congratulates himself. "I won't be late home my darling – Should be around 4'ish," he tells her while finishing off his breakfast.

"Eat up, Dianna; your lovely cooking will be going cold." And he watches as she obediently picks up her knife and fork to do his bidding. "Yes, very good, very good indeed."

Feeling on top of the world, Alex goes off to charm the world and everyone in it.

For Dianna the day passes in a haze, she moves like an automaton with no mind of her own. But as time passes a few thoughts start to assemble and cause her to stop what she's doing to try and make sense of them. Most often it is in vain, but sometimes...

Lucas...kind...horses...horses...love Lucas...

A tear slips from her dull eyes as vague longing moves through her. But then it is gone and the veil of fog clouds her thoughts again.

By the time Alex comes home the length of time when Dianna's thoughts become clearer has gotten longer, but she pretends to be just as stupefied as when he left that morning.

When he leans down to kiss her Dianna lifts her cheek in a docile manner that seems to please Alex, then she takes his coat and hangs it in the hall closet.

"Well now, isn't this lovely," Alex beams, delighted that Dianna seems to be fitting into her new role admirably. "I usually enjoy a brandy after a hard day's work, perhaps you could remember that for tomorrow?" he prompts with a raised brow.

"Yes, yes I will," Dianna tells him, the tone of her voice as flat and expressionless as her face.

Frowning, Alex moves into the sitting room and takes a seat, watching as Dianna follows him like a puppy dog. "The brandy is over there," and he points to a beautiful sideboard atop which sits a silver tray with two crystal carafes, one containing whiskey and the other brandy.

Moving silently across the room, Dianna pours the brandy into one of the beautifully cut glasses and carries it back to Alex.

"Take a seat, Dianna," he snaps out, irritated by the lack of conversation or any other interaction. "I need to get the level of your medication right – it won't do for you to walk round like a damned robot all the time," he moans and takes a sip of the exquisite brandy. "It's not like I enjoy having to medicate you, I quite enjoyed our little outings when you were more lucid. But you need to learn your place and I can't trust you to do as you're told without the meds."

Watching her, seeing that his words haven't made even the slightest difference to her expression, Alex gets to his feet and crosses to replenish his brandy glass. "I mean, if you had only turned to me as I'd planned when you miscarried the baby, none of this would have been necessary."

Planned? You planned for me to turn to you...but how...how could you plan...unless...

It is only by drawing on her deeply entrenched survival instincts that Dianna is able to maintain her docile demeanour while inside her head she is screaming with the realisation.

You took my baby! Somehow you caused me to lose my child. But how...?

"I have to admit, I was dubious that Mifepristone alone would do the trick, so I gave you a larger dose and added another little cocktail to guarantee success."

"I actually did you a huge favour," Alex continues. "Can you imagine the life you would have had bringing up that brat on your own? No, no, it doesn't bear contemplation. Just think about the life we will have together now that you have finally seen sense," Alex continues, appearing to convince himself as much as trying to convince Dianna. "Now, any thoughts on dinner...I could eat a horse!"

CHAPTER EIGHTEEN

The drive to Birmingham has been long and slow, the motorways almost coming to a standstill at times. But Lucas is determined to speak to Melinda Parker in person and find out what he can about Alex Harvey's intrusion into her life.

Pulling up outside of an old converted warehouse building, Lucas looks up at the top floor and wonders what he'll find.

She'd been reluctant to meet with him at first, had put the phone down on him repeatedly. But once she realised that he wasn't going away, Melinda had finally agreed to talk but only if he came to her.

Entering the smart lobby, Lucas looks around and then makes his way over to the lift.

He must have paid her off big time for Melinda to be

able to afford to live here. No wonder she doesn't want to rock the boat – I wonder if he's still paying?

When he steps out of the lift on the top floor, he looks around a private area that is decked out to the same high standards as the lobby had been. Crossing to the only door, Lucas presses the bell and waits.

A disembodied voice asks, "Yes, who is it?"

"It's Lucas Forrester, Ms Parker. We arranged to meet this morning."

A dull buzz sounds and the door clicks open allowing Lucas to step inside.

Once in, Lucas has to stand a minute to take in the luxury and space before him. This is loft living taken to the extreme and would have cost a small fortune to acquire.

"You have a very lovely home," he tells Melinda as she steps towards him and takes the hand he is holding out to her.

"Yes, thank you," she smiles warily. "Won't you come in and sit down. Would you like some tea or coffee?"

"Coffee, black please," Lucas smiles, and crossing to an enormous cream leather settee, takes a seat.

A couple of minutes later he is joined by Melinda as she places two elegant cups and saucers, filled with black coffee, on the glass table in front of them.

"Now, how can I help you Mr Forrester?" Melinda asks

as she curls her feet up under her on the settee.

"I need to know about what happened between you and Alex Harvey," Lucas tells her bluntly.

"Are you a reporter?" she asks, her green eyes wary and on the alert.

"No, nothing like that," Lucas assures her, and gives Melinda a winning smile. "I came across Dr Harvey when he was caring for a female friend of mine. She came to live at my house while convalescing and Harvey visited often. He seems to have become obsessed with my friend and now she's disappeared."

"Disappeared?!" Melinda pales visibly and has to put down her cup and saucer as they begin to rattle in her hands. "And you think he has her?"

"I'm certain of it," Lucas confirms. "That's why I'm here – I need to know if she is in any immediate danger. I can't get the police to act because of his status and that of his father, but if you think she's in any danger I'll push to get something done, or do it myself!" Lucas states firmly.

Getting to her feet, Melinda pushes her long red hair back from her face and begins to pace back and forth. "There's nothing I can do. I can't tell you anything," she rants, her eyes darting wildly around the room. "He'll come back and make me pay if I do. You have no idea who you're dealing with...what you're dealing with!"

Moving quickly, Lucas takes her by the arms to still her frantic pacing. "Whatever you went through Dianna is going through the same things right now – you have to tell me what he's capable of, you need to tell the police what he's capable of," Lucas demands, giving her a none too gentle shake when Melinda would have backed away.

But Melinda starts to tremble badly, and Lucas pulls her into his arms to offer comfort. "Please, Melinda, you can't leave her to suffer the way you did."

"But they didn't believe me. The police didn't want to know once they heard who had been tormenting me," she cries into his broad shoulder. "Why would they believe me now? Nothing's changed."

"I'll be with you Melinda and we'll make them believe you," Lucas asserts, and determines that they won't leave the police station until some action is taken. "My friend's cousin is a police officer – if you tell him your story I'm sure he will make sure it's followed up. He already suspects that Harvey senior has paid people off to keep his son out of trouble before."

"But if Alex hears that I've spoken to them, he'll kill me. I know you think that's extreme..." she says, pulling back to look Lucas in the eyes, "...but I'm telling you, if he feels cornered and betrayed nothing is beyond him. Nothing!"

Marty listens attentively as Melinda talks about how Alex Harvey had been her doctor after a hospital admission for injuries gained during a beating by her boyfriend. Apparently he'd been attentive and kind, coming to see her even after she'd been discharged.

"I don't remember how it started; in fact, I don't remember much at all about moving out of my flat and into Harvey's house – I just came to one morning in a bedroom I didn't recognise with Harvey standing over me," Melinda recalls with a shudder.

"He was all concerned that I'd been overdoing things and was exhausted; said he'd brought me to his home to look after me." Shuddering again, Melinda has to take a moment to steel herself to tell the rest.

"I didn't realise I was being drugged at first; I put my fuzzy head down to the exhaustion and went along with everything he said. But I was suffering terrible headaches and I couldn't think straight no matter how I tried and he would give me medication for the headache and the fuzziness would increase."

"That's when I worked out that he was drugging me," Melinda looks from Lucas to Marty, who is rapidly taking down her statement.

"Did he physically harm you, other than the drugs?" Marty asks, pen paused over the paper in front of him.

"No, as long as I did as I was told Harvey praised me and bought me expensive gifts. He said we were going to have a wonderful life together, that he would teach me how to be the perfect wife," Melinda recalls, a tear sliding down her pale face.

"But he wasn't always kind, was he?" Lucas asks gently, his soft brown voice soothing her nerves.

"No, he wasn't. If I didn't do something exactly as he wanted, or if I questioned what he'd asked me to do, he would change into this cold, hard-eyed monster who managed to scare me to death without so much as raising his voice," Melinda chokes out, the tears falling faster now.

"He'd make me do things, humiliating things as a punishment, said it was part of the training and that I should be grateful to him for taking the time to show me how to be a proper wife, a wife he could be proud of."

Taking the box of tissues that a female officer is holding out to her, Melinda wipes her eyes and blows her nose then sits up straight to continue her tale.

"It was worse when the drugs were wearing off and he did those things to me – when I was foggy brained I could zone out and pretend it wasn't me he had ordered to strip and stand naked on a chair in the kitchen while he ate a meal. But when I started to become more aware, it was awful and it shamed me to see him look at me like a piece of meat."

Pulling another tissue from the box, Melinda stems a new flood of tears and takes another moment to compose herself.

"Did he force himself on you?" Marty asks, edging a glass of cold water that the female officer has supplied nearer to Melinda.

Taking a long gulp of the welcome liquid, Melinda shakes her head and turns to the officer and says, "Could I have another glass," then polishes off the last of the water.

"Sex didn't seem to be a priority for Harvey, and none of his punishments were physical, though the threat was always there," Melinda explains. "He had a room with whips and manacles in it and a table stood in the middle of the room — Harvey told me to use my imagination about what he could do to me in there and then double it because he had a more creative mind and would do things I couldn't conceive of. And you'd better believe he was telling the truth," Melinda attests earnestly.

"Most of the time he used humiliation and mind games to get my cooperation, so much so that I became terrified of getting something wrong, of not performing whatever task it was to his standard of perfection. In the end he only had to frown to have me wetting myself with fear." And she looks from Lucas to Marty and to the female officer who hands her a fresh glass of cold water. "That's no exaggeration. I literally wet myself where I stood a couple of times, then I learned not to lose control...the punishment for messing up his pristine floor was to make me clean it with my tongue."

Chuckling derisively at their collective grimaces, Melinda continues, "It wasn't just the fact that I was being forced to drink my own urine that was so awful, it was the way he stood over me and smiled telling me that he was teaching me a lesson for my own good, that it was my fault I was being punished...and in the end I believe him..."

"Jesus..." Lucas breathes out angrily. "And you think he'll be using the same tactics on Dianna?"

Nodding, Melinda takes a sip of water and says, "I'm sure of it. He enjoyed it too much to change his tactics. Though he might drug her more than he did me – that's how I escaped," she tells them with a sneering smile. "He didn't like that I was so slow witted and couldn't hold an intelligent conversation. So he started lowering the dosage of whatever he was giving me and gradually I started to be able to think through the fog in my head. But I had to hide that fact; pretend to be more docile than

I was so as he wouldn't up the dosage again."

"Not that I was thinking clearly. Later, after I got back to my apartment and the drugs really wore off, I put it down to survivor's instinct that had me acting in just the right way," Melinda confesses.

"When I first got away from him, while I was still in the grounds, it hit me what I'd done and I was so scared I almost went back before he could find out that I'd escaped. I was so sure that he'd find me and the punishment would be even more terrible than anything he'd done before; I'd end up tied to that table, in what I thought of as the torture room, and who knows what he would have done..."

"You can't imagine how hard it was to make myself continue to flee; his hold on me was so all consuming. I was fighting myself constantly, looking over my shoulder every couple of seconds imagining his face if he found me, convinced that he would."

"It took me a whole week of locking myself in my flat and barricading the bedroom door all the time, for me to get up the courage to go to the police and tell them a version of what Harvey had done to me," Melinda sighs heavily and rubs her sore eyes.

"It wasn't that I needed to settle myself or to let the drugs work their way out of my system – it was the opposite, in fact. My terror became so absolute that going to the police became the less frightening option.

"Being in my flat waiting hour by hour, day by terrifying day, was like torture of a whole other kind. All I had to drink was tap water from the en-suite shower-room and food was just a bag of sweets I had in my bedside draw. It didn't matter what kind of hunger gripped my gut, no food was worth the risk of leaving my bedroom to go to the kitchen."

A terrible silence haunts the room until Lucas finally asks, "How long did he hold you captive?"

"A month. One very long and terrifying month – but it might as well have been a year...a lifetime for all the damage he did," Melinda blows out a long breath and finishes the second glass of water. "I'm still having therapy, and the irony is he's paying for it," she laughs bitterly. "I don't know whether the police ever took me seriously enough to actually go and confront Harvey, but his solicitor arrived on my doorstep a few days later with a fat cheque that he insisted was for services rendered, and made me sign some form to that effect."

"A payoff," Marty murmurs, pushing a hand back through his tousled blond hair as he slumps back in his chair.

"Yes, one I almost tore up. But then I started to think

about what he'd done to me and the fact that the police weren't about to do anything, and I decided that he needed to pay, even if it was only money. I hated to think he was getting off scot free!"

Pushing his chair back noisily, Lucas begins to pace the interview room, fists clenched at his sides. "The police can't do nothing and leave Dianna in that mad man's hands," he protests vehemently. "You've heard what he's capable of, and Melinda's probably forgotten the half of it due to the drugs he gave her — we need to act now," Lucas states, slamming his hands down flat on the table, bringing his face within an inch of Marty's.

"Back off," Marty demands, his voice dangerously soft, his dark brown eyes not leaving Lucas'.

For a moment the two men stare each other down, then Lucas slowly moves back and retakes his seat next to Melinda.

The female officer returns to her position at the door, having moved forward in case her boss needed assistance. But her demeanour tells Lucas that she is ready for him should he make a wrong move.

Looking back to Melinda, Marty asks her to wait while he goes and talks to his boss. "It shouldn't take long, but I want you to be available in case he has any questions for you. Ok?"

When Melinda gives him a nod, Marty departs the room leaving the female officer still at the door.

"I know we're not under arrest..." Melinda whispers to Lucas, "...but it sure as hell feels like it."

A few minutes later and Marty is back, the word has been given and the word is, Go! Go! Go!

Finally, alone in her room Dianna is able to grieve for her baby. Rocking herself on the bed, her tears are silent lest Alex Harvey hear her.

The sobs that rack her body now are as bad as the cramping pains that Dianna had suffered at the time of the miscarriage; such is the depth of her grief.

It is a kindness when she falls into a dreamless sleep, aided by the drugged wine that Harvey had insisted she drink during dinner.

Outside the wrought iron gates, a small army of police is gathered ready to storm the house and come to her rescue. Blissfully unaware, Dianna sinks into a welcome oblivion.

After working to bypass the remote controlled gates, the police move forward – Marty in the lead and Lucas bringing up the rear.

Stealthily they approach the house then one of them moves forward with a battering ram.

Holding a hand up to get everyone's attention, Marty

turns to the man holding the battering ram and holds up three fingers, then he slowly lowers one at a time and gives the officer the nod to go ahead.

From that moment on everything moves quickly, like a movie on fast forward. Alex comes charging out of the sitting room, a glass of brandy still in hand, protesting loudly about the intrusion.

"You have no right to be here," Alex tells Marty after the detective has read out the charges against him and informed Alex of his rights.

"You can't touch me..." Alex sneers down his nose at Lucas when he comes into the house behind the other officers, "...I have more money than God and when my father hears about this..."

Before anyone has any idea about what he is about to do, Lucas pushes forward and rams his fist into Alex's smarmy face then gives a satisfied laugh when he crumples to the floor unconscious.

"You little shit!" Lucas stands over the unmoving man then turns his eyes to Marty. "Has anyone gone to look for Dianna?"

"My men are on it," Marty nods. "You realise he might press charges," he continues, referring to Alex.

"It was worth it!" Lucas proclaims, turning away to join the search for Dianna.

A call goes up and Lucas heads in the direction it came from. Taking the stairs two at a time, he follows a couple of other officers along the landing.

"She's here..." an officer tells him when he enters the bedroom, "...looks to be out of it, but no obvious sign of external injuries."

"Let me get to her," Lucas insists, pushing past the men in his way.

When a pair of large hands shake her awake, Dianna fears that Harvey is angry, that he is about to take her to 'that room'. He's threatened to do so many times, and now she is sure that it's about to happen.

"No, please, please don't," she cries, her voice unable to express the desperation she is feeling within, her mind dull with sleep and the effects of the drugs. "I'll be good...I'll do better..."

"Dianna! Wake up! Oh Christ, don't cry...baby please don't cry," Lucas pulls Dianna onto his lap and wraps warm strong arms about her, rocking her gently.

Still not able to understand what is going on, Dianna sinks into Lucas' embrace believing that she is lost in an amazingly real dream. She can not only hear his voice and feel his warmth, she can smell all that is Lucas and breaths him in deeply. "Lucas, I was so stupid...such a coward...should have told you...wanted to tell you..." she mutters, her words slurred and dreamy sounding.

"What did you want to tell me, my darling?" Lucas croons into her dishevelled hair.

"That I love you...course," she tells him, and snuggles deeper into what has to be the best dream she's ever had.

<u>EPILOGUE</u>

Four months later and Dianna is a changed woman. Her confidence is gradually returning and she and Lucas are planning their wedding.

Only one cloud still lingers on the horizon.

"I'm just glad the trial will be over with before the wedding," Dianna sighs, her smile only slightly hesitant. "I don't want that scum to ruin our day."

"He won't," Lucas states firmly. "Even daddy's money couldn't buy Harvey out of the trouble he's in now. Your statement was damning in the extreme, and the blood tests the hospital took proved what medication he'd given you, as well as the stock of them they found in his house. He'd been stealing them from the hospital, bit by bit. That in itself will get him time."

"Yes, and they found the drugs he gave me to induce

the miscarriage. I will never be able to forgive him for that, even if they do diagnose him with a mental disorder," Dianna frowns, picking up her cup to sip some tea.

"Hmm, seems like that's the likely outcome. Marty told Hank that the psychiatrists are preparing their reports. Harvey senior has paid thousands for someone to put the best spin possible on the situation," Lucas tells her reluctantly. "But the prosecutor has brought in a major player of his own, someone with a much respected reputation."

"I'm not looking forward to testifying, and neither is Melinda – did I tell you that her mother has moved in with her," Dianna asks. "Apparently she's been very supportive and Melinda has told her family everything. She said she'd felt too ashamed to tell them before, but now she's just happy it's all out in the open and wants to make Harvey pay."

"Let's forget about Harvey for now and go for a walk," Lucas tells her, reaching for Dianna's hand.

"Ok," she smiles, happy to let the past go for a while.

Arm in arm they walk through the garden and out to the large field at the back. A new stable block has just been completed, along with an outdoor training ring and a tack room plus a small barn is still under construction.

"There's still a lot to do before the horses arrive..." Lucas tells her, "...but that should pan out nicely for when we get back from our honeymoon."

He still hasn't told her where he's taking her and will only say that it will be hot, dry and beautiful.

But Dianna doesn't care where they go as long as she is with Lucas.

Having watched the construction from a distance, this is the first time that Dianna has been allowed to walk round the completed structures.

"I should make you wear a blindfold," Lucas laughs as they approach the stables. "Like one of those TV shows when they do 'the big reveal'." And they both laugh at the idea.

"Well it's not like I haven't watched it all going up, but I must admit I'm excited to see it up close," Dianna beams, her dream of running her own riding school so close to being real now.

"Are you still happy with your decision to sell the cottage?" he asks. He had wanted Dianna to wait, to rent it out for a while and make a clear-headed decision.

But Dianna had insisted, wanting to free herself from her past and invest all the proceeds in her future.

"I couldn't be happier," she assures him. "You've been good enough to let me use the land rent free, but I wanted to pay for the buildings and the horses myself. I won't be able to buy all the horses I want right away, but in time the business will grow and then I'll be able to take on a helper."

Walking into one of the stalls, Lucas stands back to watch Dianna enjoy the moment. Her eyes are round and dart from corner to corner, planning what will go where.

"This rubber flooring is brilliant – comfortable for the horses to lay on and cost effective in the long run. And a lot less labour intensive to keep clean," Dianna observes, jumping up and down to test it out.

"I'll need to get rounded hooks put in the corners, about here," she points, "...for the hay nets to hang on." But then she shakes her head, causing her waist length auburn hair to shimmer down her back, "No, scratch that, we'll go for heavy duty hayracks – they're more expensive but will pay for themselves in time. And I'll need a few feeding buckets – I prefer the rubber ones, they're almost indestructible and easy to keep clean."

Catching her to him, Lucas turns Dianna in his arms and claims her lips, effectively shutting her up.

One minute her head is filled with lists of essentials that she has yet to order, the next her mind is on Lucas and the pleasures he can give her.

With hands flat against the hard muscles of his chest,

Dianna feels his thudding heart and loves that she has this effect on him.

When his tongue probes and tastes, sweeping against her lips like he can't get enough of her, she opens to him willingly finding the sensation so erotic.

Every time they make love is like the first time, with all the bells and whistles going off in her head, her body responding to his touch like dry tinder to the heat of the sun. Flames flick over her skin, searing through her and causing her to gasp out loud.

And Lucas loves to hear those little moans, knowing that she can't prevent their escape, can't contain her pleasure at the needs and sensations he rouses in her time and time again.

Without fumbling, his fingers begin to undo buttons and clips, undressing her whilst caressing her skin, her naked breasts and following his hands with his lips and teeth. "God, you taste so good," he groans, lowering Dianna to the rubber flooring.

The first time they made love, Dianna had felt guilt as well as passion. A sense that she was betraying her husband, was cheating on him, had cast a shadow but it hadn't lasted.

Like now, their bond had drawn them together, touching, tasting, leading them down a path filled with carnal pleasure. And that shadow has never returned, it has been eradicated by the pureness of their love, their depth of belonging to each other and their desire to spend the rest of their lives within the other's embrace.

He couldn't kiss her deeply enough, couldn't touch her intimate places long enough, gently enough, roughly enough. She would give him everything, allow him anything he desired, but still it would never be enough.

When she is naked to his eyes, they feast hungrily and he moves his lithe body over hers.

She hadn't realised that he'd also gotten naked; his hands had never seemed to leave her. But she is glad and eager to feel him inside her, to know that he craves this as much as she.

Her breath eases out on a sigh that seems to come from the core of her being, the length of him filling her in a long, slow slide that makes her feel whole.

As her nails rake down his back, Lucas lets loose a growl that thrills her inner woman and has her fingers digging into his taught buttocks to pull him back into her every time he moves away.

Their rhythm grows along with the need to be as one, joining in a furore of heat and passion that might consume them at any moment.

"More! More!" Lucas growls, his hips now pistoning

his hard length into her so deeply Dianna wonders if it's possible to die from the pleasures now erupting from within.

The crest isn't a gentle rise and fall, but is more of an explosion of mind, heart and body that has them gasping for air in order to survive it.

Lying together, still joined, still coming down from the great heights of ecstasy their bodies had reached, Dianna smiles into Lucas' chest, thinking about the baby they have recently discovered is growing inside of her, made by just such an act of love.

"Will you still want me when I'm all fat and swollen," she asks Lucas, kissing his still shuddering chest just because she can't resist.

"I'll always want you. I'll want you even when we're both old and grey, when we have to use a Zimmer frame to get about," he chuckles, then dips his head to kiss her swollen lips. "If I'm still breathing I'll find the strength from somewhere to be inside you because that's where I belong."

*****

If you have enjoyed this book please leave a review at the point of purchase.